Becky rested on Kevin's broad chest, her head bent to his lips with the answer he demanded. He met her halfway, his soft mouth coaxing her to follow him into a sensuous world Becky realized she had missed for so long. The feeling of his strong hands on her back, his breathing beneath her, the contrasting softness of his lips and the harsher texture of his mustache and beard immersed her in a pool of sensations she savored. For tonight, it was enough to hold each other, to lie together, listening to the night sounds. talking softly and watching the lamplight flicker over their bodies. From Kevin's responses Becky wondered how long he would be comfortable with her leisurely approach. For that matter, how long would she?

Dear Reader,

We're so proud to bring you Harlequin
Intrigue. These books blend adventure and
excitement with the compelling love stories
you've come to associate with Harlequin.

This series is unique; it combines
contemporary themes with the fast-paced
action of a good old-fashioned page turner.
You'll identify with these spirited, realistic
heroines as they seek the answers, flirting
with both danger and passion along the way.

We hope you'll enjoy these new books,
and we look forward to your comments
and suggestions.

The Editors
Harlequin Intrigue
919 Third Avenue
New York, N.Y. 10022

RAINBOW RIBBON
PAMELA THOMPSON

Harlequin Books

TORONTO • NEW YORK • LONDON
AMSTERDAM • PARIS • SYDNEY • HAMBURG
STOCKHOLM • ATHENS • TOKYO • MILAN

"...a vision of some gay creatures of the element
That in the colours of the rainbow live."

—*Milton*

To all "creatures that in the colours of the rainbow live"
and especially to The Beginning People, who first believed
in our rainbow and its kettle of dreams.

Harlequin Intrigue edition published November 1984

ISBN 0-373-22007-3

Chapter One

Pipe threads creaked like a basso katydid as the two men connected the big conduit to the brass valve nearly hidden in the tall grass. The sound seemed to blend with the more natural night symphony of summer. Even the burbling sound of liquid cascading down the hill as the older man opened the valve might have been mistaken for a natural occurrence.

As the older man sat back to wait, the younger man spoke in a hoarse whisper. "Damn it, Charley, I don't like this. What we're doing is illegal. What if we get caught?"

Charley lit a cigarette, carefully extinguishing the match between his finger and thumb. "We're not gonna get caught. Besides, we're only doing what we're getting paid to do."

The other man whispered with fierce intensity. "Listen, man, you know who'll get hung out to dry if anything goes wrong...and it won't be the boss."

"Why are you whispering?" Charley's voice seemed to boom in the heavy darkness. "There's nobody around for miles."

"You better hope that's true," Leo insisted nervously.

"Relax, Leo. We're getting double overtime for three hours' work, and it isn't gonna take much over an hour here. That's pretty easy money, seems to me."

Leo snapped off a nearby weed and began breaking it into small pieces. "What if somebody complains, Charley? What happens then?"

"Leo, it's Friday night," Charley said patiently. "Who's gonna complain? You know government people don't work weekends. By Monday morning, all this will be twenty miles downstream and forgotten."

"I still don't like it," Leo persisted stubbornly. "We've never dumped like this before. Why can't we run it through the city sewer like we always have?"

"Because Oakdale's new standards for how much we can put into their system are higher than they used to be. We're overloaded on this stuff. They check us pretty close, so it has to go somewhere. The sludge pond is brimming."

"So why don't they have it hauled off somewhere?"

Charley laughed ruefully. "You got a lot to learn about industry, kid. Those waste haulers charge an arm and a leg to pick up the stuff, and they'd probably do the same thing we're doing: Dump it in the first creek or ditch they came to. So why pay out all that money for no better results? Boss pays them for paperwork saying they picked it up; easy money for them, and it solves our problem."

Leo stood and looked around frowning. "I'll still be glad when we're through."

"Leo, it's not like we're dumping mercury or something really bad. This is just run-of-the-mill factory soup; no heavy metals or outright poisons."

"Doesn't smell like any soup I'd be interested in eating...or drinking," Leo muttered.

"Trust me, kid," Charley said, getting to his feet. "There's nothing in this soup that's gonna hurt anybody. By Monday morning, at the rate water moves in that creek, nobody will ever know it was there."

Leo lapsed into an uneasy silence until the burble died to a trickle. At Charley's signal, they quickly and quietly disconnected the big pipe and carried it back to the waiting truck, their overtime earned and the weekend still ahead of them.

One of the few things Becky Sherman enjoyed more than waking up on a bright summer morning at Rainbow Ribbon Trout Farm was knowing it was Sunday and she could stay in bed a little longer. The restaurant was closed on Sundays, and the only other thing she really had to do today was help her father move fingerling trout to a new pond. Knowing that could be done in the afternoon, she turned away from the window streaming sunlight, punched her pillow into a more comfortable configuration, and settled into it again.

The mauve mists of near-sleep had barely enwrapped her when the shrill scream of the telephone jarred her like an electric shock, speeding up her heart and rearranging her striking features into a irritated scowl. Who would have the temerity to be calling her early on a Sunday morning? Before it could ring a second time, Becky snatched the receiver from its cradle. "Hello?"

"Rebecca, you have to come help us right away.

Hurry!'' Frances Sherman's voice was as shrill as the telephone bell.

"Mother, what is it? What's the matter?" For a split second her soft turquoise eyes widened with fear that something had happened to her father, then she grabbed her mother's use of the word " ıs" for security. "Calm down, Mother. Tell me what's wrong."

"It's the fish, Rebecca," her mother's voice broke. "They're dying. The fish are all dying. You have to come help us with them right away."

"Dying? What's...." The receiver went dead as her mother broke the connection abruptly.

Now fully awake, Becky ran to her window and looked down at the trout ponds in the valley below. She could see her dad's truck, and two figures racing around. Hastily she slipped her slender, lightly tanned legs into cutoffs and sneakers and grabbed a T-shirt off the chair, pulling it over her head as she headed down the stairs from her apartment through the deserted restaurant. She quickly decided the fastest way to the ponds would be to drive, so she jumped into her car and whipped down the driveway past her parents' home and around the loop leading to the trout ponds. Long before she reached the valley she could see the dull gleam of white bellies that live trout never showed.

As Becky leaped from the car, she could see her father in waders hip deep in one of the ponds, scooping up fish while his German shepherd, Major, ran up and down the banks impotently. The raceway screens were clogged with dead and dying fish as the swift water strained to rid itself of the devastation. Instead of lovely dappled fish streaking through the cool waters,

Becky saw piles of stricken trout gasping for air or, their struggles futile, lying flaccidly as their rainbows faded into the grim chalkiness of death. For a moment Becky stood gasping, too, trying to accommodate the horror that confronted her. "Dad, what happened?" she finally managed to croak as she reached the pond bank.

Gene Sherman's blue eyes were shadowed by the billed cap, but his face was pale. "I don't know, honey, but we have to get them out of here as quickly as possible. We have to save all we can." He continued scooping trout onto the bank. "Anything still breathing, put it in one of the cans there." He indicated large plastic garbage cans collected from all over the farm. "We'll process them for the freezer as soon as we can."

"What's the status in the other ponds?" Becky asked. "Are all the fish dead?"

Gene shook his head. "No, at least not yet. When I came down to feed them, some were already dead and the others were showing signs of suffocation. I started the aeration pumps, but I don't know whether they put enough oxygen into the water to do any good. It has to help, though, and I don't know what else to do."

"Dad, come out for a minute and let's get organized," Becky pleaded as her mind whirled. She ran her fingers through her sleep-touseled chestnut hair as if she could as easily smooth the tangles in her mind. "Do you have any idea what killed them?"

Gene waded wearily out of the pond, patiently fending off his dog's anxious attentions. Major was Gene's constant companion and sensitive to his master's distresses because of their relative infrequency. "Lack of oxygen killed them, Beck, but I have no idea what either consumed or blocked off all the oxygen. I suppose it could be some kind of poison, but they weren't behaving as if they were poisoned...no nervous-system symptoms. They were frantically gasping for air at the surface, as if they were smothering, as if someone had laid a giant plastic bag over the pond. When the oxygen in the water was gone, they simply suffocated.'' He shook himself from his dreadful reverie. ''Whatever did it, they're fresh enough to process and safe enough to eat. Your mother is calling people to come help us with them.''

''Dad, why are we dressing them when we don't even know what killed them? What if it was something toxic?''

Gene looked at Becky, his face gray and drawn. ''For now, you'll have to rely on my judgment, Beck. Have them tested later if you want, but we have to do something right now. You're looking at time, money, and food going to waste unless we do something, Becky. Nothing like this has ever happened here... not in thirty years of fish farming. What else can we do?''

Becky realized her father was coping in his own way by trying to salvage something from the disaster, by staying busy to avoid the overwhelming realization of what had happened. She hugged him impulsively. ''If Mother is calling for help, I think I'll collect some fish and water samples so we can have them checked tomorrow, okay?''

''Oh, yeah...that's a good idea,'' her father said dazedly as he turned again to the gruesome harvest of fish he had raised from eggs, tended for two years only to end in this uselss debacle. Major resumed his patrolling of the piles of dead fish.

Becky cursed the timing as she rummaged through the hatchery building cabinets for clean glass jars used for water sampling. It would be easier to walk across the surface of the pond than to find anyone from the health department or Pollution Control on a Sunday. She ran to the far end of the pond and scooped up water samples below the clogged fish screen. The speed of water movement in the raceways might work against identifying the pollutant, she thought bleakly, but it was worth a try. She gathered up several dead trout and stuck them in the refrigerator of the processing shed. Dead so recently, the rainbow markings of the fish were already fading. Becky remembered her father telling her when she was a child that fish had chemical factories inside them to make all those pretty colors. It didn't take long for the factories to shut down, she thought ironically. She had grown up with rainbow trout, fed the fingerlings when her hands were too small to hold the big pellets, used their graceful beauty as a readily available tranquilizer during the traumas of adolescence, learned to treasure the water and its denizens. As Becky watched the lovely colors fade, a rage began to grow in her gut. If this had never happened in thirty years on this farm, then somebody must have done something to cause it.

As she stalked toward the pond to help her father, Becky determined tomorrow would be spent tracking down whoever was responsible for this carnage. As she sorted fish, her agile mind sorted ideas and planned the steps she would take.

Cars began pulling into the lot as family friends arrived in response to Frances's call for help. After the initial shock, they set up an assembly line to retrieve, sort, and dress the fish. One crew slit the fish open and removed the entrails, while a second crew washed the gutted fish and put them in plastic bags, scales and heads intact. It was a grim task, and the usually chatty friends were unusually quiet as they worked.

When they broke for a lunch prepared by Frances and Becky, they had made a considerable dent in the number of fish, but it was obvious they wouldn't be able to deal with them all. Gene admitted privately to Becky he wasn't sure he would be able to find storage or markets for all of them anyway.

By late afternoon Gene called a halt to the salvage operation, sending the crew home with as many trout as they could use or give to friends and relatives and storing several days' worth for the restaurant, after they were approved for use. After everyone else left, Gene and Becky drove to the back pasture to locate a burying site for the remainder.

When they returned, Frances had soup and sandwiches waiting for them. They ate in an exhausted silence. As they sipped at mugs of hot coffee, Becky decided to compare her plans with her father's thinking about the incident.

"Dad, we have to report this tomorrow. Who do we call first?"

"I honestly don't know," her dad said and shrugged. "We've never had a need to know until now."

"Well, I guess the health department would test the fish—"

"I think they're okay," Frances interjected. "I didn't see any tissue damage when we were dressing them . . . nothing out of the ordinary at all."

"More importantly," Becky continued, "we have to get Pollution Control or somebody to help us track down the cause. If we don't find out what caused it, we could wake up to another morning like this one. I don't know about you, but I don't think I could take many days like this one has been."

"Could be anything," Gene replied quietly. "Somebody could have spilled something toxic up the ridge, miles from here. You know how stuff travels through this rocky ground."

Gene Sherman was a calm man by nature, able to accept life's vagaries with equanimity. His daughter inherited his deep blue-green eyes, but her nature was her own and as volatile as his was placid. "Dad," she said angrily, "we've lost at least five thousand fish today and more than an equal number of dollars. Damn it, you can't afford to be philosophical about that kind of loss, especially when we have no assurance it won't happen again. I'm going to spend tomorrow on the phone until I find someone who can help us."

Becky's mother frowned anxiously. "Rebecca, the last thing we want is a lot of publicity about something being wrong with Rainbow Ribbon trout. It's never happened before, so it seems likely to me that your father's right: it's probably a one-time accident. Now you know how you are when you get geared up; you never know where to stop. I'm sure your father is right."

Becky recognized her mother's speech as part of her

endless campaign to stamp out any sort of conflict, healthy or otherwise. "Mother," she said impatiently, "the fact that it never happened before leads me to a different conclusion, that it may be the first of many times. Somebody somewhere did something that ended up costing us a lot of money and pain. That someone should be found and made to pay."

"Becky, all you'll do is bring a lot of people in here poking around; they won't find anything, and they'll go away thinking our fish are diseased or something. That won't help the farm or the restaurant, you know. Your father knows what to do. Let him handle it."

Becky flared, her deep eyes flashing in frustration. "You just heard him say he didn't know what to do, Mother. There are laws about pollution, laws that are designed to protect people like us from people like whoever did this. I have my life savings in that restaurant up there, and I need a very secure source of good quality trout, don't I? I have a legitimate interest in this, too, don't I?"

"Of course, you do, honey," her father intervened, "and I think it's fine for you to do what you can to find out what happened. Just don't be surprised if you get a less than enthusiastic response from the people you talk to. The laws may be designed to protect us, but it's people we'll have to depend on to make those laws worth the paper they're written on. The people who pollute are generally more influential than the people at this end of the pipe."

"My daddy the cynic." She grinned wryly, rising to leave before the argument with her mother escalated further. "I'll do some calling around in the morning and see if you're right, doubting Thomas. G'night."

Becky stood in the shower for a long time, scrubbing the fishy smell from her slender body and the weariness from her bones. She was in pretty good physical condition, but it had been a long, awful day and it could be just the beginning. For the first time in the three years since she opened Rainbow's End, the restaurant was showing a real profit and signs of the success she envisioned for it. If her customers got wind of a mysterious fish kill...she didn't really want to think about that.

She dried herself quickly and crawled into bed, the full import of the day closing in around her. Becky had been so sure coming back to the Ozark highlands had put the horrors of city life behind her, including the industrial pollution that stained the skies and killed the rivers. "Guess again, girl," she said with an audible sigh. She thought she was through with crusading, but what she had experienced this day would put the necessary starch back in her spine. She had too much to lose to leave it to some anonymous beneficence.

It didn't take long for sleep to numb Becky's racing mind and still her fatigued body, but her dreams weren't restful. Although she was running as fast as she could, a sea of dead white trout continued to spill over the banks and rise around her ankles as Rainbow's End slumped and slid into the slimy waters from which all life had gone.

Chapter Two

The hot, yellow sun pained Becky's bleary eyes when she woke Monday morning, and for a moment she couldn't remember whether the fish kill was real or a dream. When she moved, her protesting muscles informed her in no uncertain terms of the reality of yesterday's marathon. She dragged herself out of bed, wanting to be dressed and breakfasted by the time government offices opened. If her dad was correct, it could be a long day, so she decided to get an early start.

At the stroke of nine, Becky dialed the first number on her list of possible agencies. The first agency politely referred her to another, which indifferently indicated a third might be interested, where she finally got the number of an inspector at the State Pollution Control Agency in the state capital. After hearing Becky's explanation of the situation, he assured her he would send someone out to check on it. He promised to call by early afternoon to tell her when she might expect a visit and suggested she might check with the city of Oakdale about any possible spills of toxic materials. She thanked him and took the receiver, by now warm and clammy with constant use, from her throbbing ear.

Tired of sitting and even more tired of the telephone, Becky decided she would drive to town to brave city hall. First, she had to call Sheila to cover for her at the restaurant. Sheila Marlowe was Becky's childhood chum and good right arm. If Becky had to spend the day chasing bureaucrats, Sheila would need to see to preparations for the evening business at Rainbow's End. She dialed her friend's number.

"Hi, Sandy," she greeted Sheila's teenage daughter. "Could I speak to your mom, please? Thanks."

"Morning, boss." Sheila's rich, warm tones filled Becky's ears. "What can I do for you so early on a Monday?"

Becky quickly outlined Sunday's disaster and her plan for the day. "I'm leaving now to see if I can find out anything at city hall. If the rest of the day is like this morning, I may not be back in time to get everything lined up for dinner. You do it as well as I do, so would you mind coming in early to cover for me?"

"Do you even have to ask?" Sheila groaned sympathetically. "Poor Gene. How's he taking it?"

"Too calmly, for my money," Becky retorted quickly.

"No sense in both of you getting excited," Sheila commented on Becky's agitation. "Don't give it another thought, Becky. Tell Gene to hang in there, and I'll see you when you get here. Should I bring a shawl?"

Becky laughed. "I don't think so. I won't be that late, Sheila. Thanks, love." Becky chuckled at her friend's question. When Sheila did hostess duties at the restaurant, she wore gowns from Becky's considerable wardrobe of glamour rags acquired during her ten-year career as a lobbyist in Washington, D.C. Becky was glad to get some use from them, and Sheila wore the same size clothing. However, Sheila never felt comfortable with the sexy cut of the gowns, so she had amassed a wardrobe of stoles and shawls that matched Becky's gowns. How two people of the same size could look so different in the same gown was a long-standing joke between them.

Becky brushed her thick brown hair behind her ears and stuck combs into it. She was cooler with her hair off her face, but she was not unaware of the fine bone structure accentuated by the style. She stuck her lucky turquoise drops into her earlobes, thinking she shouldn't pass up any possible advantage, and the deep color of her eyes glowed to match the nearby stones. Becky was a good-looking woman by any standards, and while she knew it, she neither relied on it nor traded on it. Because she accepted herself, feeling her looks were largely an accident of genetics, she gained initial acceptance from more people than the average beautiful woman.

She dropped by her parents' house to tell them where she was going and that Sheila would be in early. Major greeted her at the door with his usual enthusiasm. "I see you, big dog. How could I not see something your size?" She grinned as she pounded his broad back. "Anybody home?" she called, sticking her head through the kitchen door.

Frances was in the laundry room. "Your father is burying fish, Becky," she said, walking into sight with a stack of folded towels, each of which Becky suspected was used only once before laundering. Her mother was a fastidious woman who needed to make work for herself after her children left home. "Looks as if he saved quite a few, though, by turning on the aerators when he did. Bless his heart," she clucked, "it's not just the money. You know how he feels about those fish."

"I know," Becky said. "I hope he called George to help him with it."

"He did," her mother confirmed. "It'll still be hard for him. Have you found out anything yet?"

"I'm on my way to city hall now, and Pollution Control in Little Rock says they'll send someone soon," she related briefly. "Not soon enough, I suspect. Listen, I've called Sheila to come in early in case I get held up somewhere, so don't worry about dinner if I'm late getting back."

"I'll see if Sheila needs any help. I could use a little diversion today," she said a trifle sadly.

"I'm sure she'll appreciate it," Becky assured her mother. "I'll see you when I get back. Maybe I'll have some good news." Becky felt less confident about that after her morning of disappointing calls, but there was no point in telling Frances of her misgivings.

It was nearly noon when she reached the parking lot at city hall. Oakdale was not a big town, but the building looked larger than usual to Becky as she considered having to wander through every office to find someone who knew or cared about her problem. She steeled herself and rehearsed the briefest possible outline of the problem, expecting to repeat it several times before someone took the bait.

The receptionist in the lobby listened with less than rapt attention to Becky's query. She seemed to have not the least idea who might be able to help her with something like that. "You might try engineering. If they can't help you, they might know who could," she offered, pointing down the hall. "Third office on the left."

"Nice to know restaurants aren't the only places who have trouble getting good help," Becky muttered to herself as she headed down the hall. "Wonder if she realizes she works for me."

At the third door on the left, Becky paused to peer into a huge room with partitioned work areas, desks scattered about it, apparently at random, and walls covered with blueprints and esoteric charts. It seemed devoid of life. She glanced at her watch and realized it was the noon hour. Terrific timing. Without genuine hope, Becky started peeking into cubbyholes for anyone in residence. As she stuck her head around the last partition, she discovered a desk supporting a pair of booted feet leading to pressed khaki pants, a red plaid shirt, and a head buried in a book. Nice hair, Becky thought, noting the jet locks streaked with white in an unusually interesting way. "Pardon me," she said apologetically, "I hate to disturb your lunch"—which seemed to be the half-eaten apple in his hand—"but I...."

The head jerked up, and Becky found herself looking over a pair of half-glasses into the bluest eyes she'd ever seen above a beard to match the hair. The combination was so striking, she simply stared until he spoke.

"Hi," the man said, pulling off the glasses and

swinging his feet off the desk, "can I help you with something?" His expression was open and friendly. He quickly gathered loose papers off the seat of the only other chair in the office. "Have a seat. I'm Kevin McClain."

"I'm Becky Sherman," she said, taking his extended hand, then collapsing into the chair in relief, "and I certainly hope you can help me, Mr. McClain."

As she related the events of the day before, Kevin sat quietly stroking his beard, his eyes never leaving her face. He nodded occasionally in sympathy or understanding or perhaps just to keep her talking. Becky couldn't be sure about that, but she was delighted to find someone who would sit face to face with her and simply listen, who didn't seem anxious to pass her on to someone else as soon as possible. "So, you see I'm not sure who or what I'm really looking for here, but Pollution Control thought maybe the city might be able to get some sort of line on where the pollution could have originated."

"I see," Kevin leaned back in his chair. "Who have you already contacted?"

Becky snorted in frustration. "Do you really want the whole sordid list?"

A slow smile rearranged Kevin's face, wreathing the startling blue eyes in laugh lines. "Sure. I've got the time if you have."

She leaned back, took a deep breath, and began the recitation. "Well, first I called the local health department. They told me the trout would have to be in my restaurant, on a plate, ready for customer consumption, before they could get involved. They're not interested in fish in the wild, but they thought probably the state agency who handles wildlife and fisheries might be. The people there told me they couldn't be interested because the fish kill took place on private property. For them to be involved, the kill has to be in a public waterway." She stopped as she noticed Kevin's head shaking and sinking toward his chest. "Am I boring you?"

He wore a rueful grin as he looked up at her. "Not in the least, Ms Sherman, but the functioning of political structures never ceases to amaze me. Our tax dollars at work," he chuckled. "Please go on."

Becky returned his easy smile and relaxed a little. "They suggested I call Pollution Control. Of course, you have to remember it's Monday morning and everybody has staff meetings on Monday mornings, right? They're supposed to get back to me this afternoon, but they suggested I contact the City of Oakdale to see if they knew of any spills or anything that might be helpful. So here I am, telling you my long, sad story and taking a chance on another rejection."

Kevin scrutinized the lovely, anxious face. "Actually, I think I may be able to help you."

The anxiety turned to astonishment. "Really?"

"Well, not in my official capacity with the city," he said, "but I only work here part-time to help pay the bills while I'm in school. As luck would have it, I'm working on an advanced degree in biology, and I'm very interested in fisheries and pollution. Maybe the city can't help, but maybe I can," he offered, rising to move toward a map on the wall. "Come show me where your farm is."

As he turned his back to her, Becky noticed the stocky fitness of his body. He certainly didn't spend all his time sitting behind a desk. She judged him to be around forty, despite the silver beginning to streak his dark hair.

"Right here." Becky pointed to the map, thinking she liked this man's style. He was direct, pleasant, and probably very interesting. She perched on the edge of his desk as he scanned the area.

"Eliminate the obvious first," he said as he searched the map. "There are no sewer lift stations in the area, so we can cross that off." He thought for a minute and turned the searching blue eyes on her. "Did you see any sudsy or oily materials on the surface of the ponds?"

"I took some water samples and kept some of the fish, but everything was so hectic, I can't say I noticed. I'm sure there couldn't have been much or someone would have noticed. My father waded around in it all day."

"Tell you what," Kevin suggested, "why don't I come out after I'm through here this afternoon and look around? I'll take some samples to the university lab." He held up a cautionary hand. "Now don't get your hopes up. We may not find a thing. Fortunately or unfortunately, depending on your point of view, fast-moving water cleanses itself pretty quickly."

"I know, but it's the best offer I've had today, Mr. McClain, so I'll take it gratefully." She stood with a fluid motion. "After you turn off the highway, just follow the signs—you can't miss us. Thanks for your time," she said, turning toward the door.

He walked with her through the maze of desks to the door. "I'll see you around four o'clock then." As he watched the slender woman walk down the hall away from him, Kevin silently thanked her for presenting him with his first real challenge since taking this job. He needed the money, but he didn't want to survey streets and sewers; he wanted to work on environmental problems. After weeks of crushing boredom, in comes a beautiful woman and lays a perfect problem in his lap. He would enjoy the challenge of searching for the problem, the satisfaction of helping people who usually got swept under the rug in these situations, and, admittedly, the stimulation of close association with a woman whose personality and intelligence seemed to match her looks. Smiling, he went back to his desk to gather up papers and charts for the meeting he knew would take the lion's share of the afternoon.

Kevin's smile had faded by the time all the members of the Waste Management Committee straggled into the conference room. Thinking how much he would prefer being at the trout farm, he listened to Gordon Yates, the mayor's administrative assistant, call the meeting to order and introduce the presenter. "We have a representative from Kendall Associates engineering firm with us this afternoon to present a proposal for the new sewage treatment plant. Mr. Kendall?"

"Thank you, Gordon," the guest said as he rose and walked toward the easel stacked with the obligatory charts. "I've prepared a few charts to show you what our company proposes...." Kevin sat doodling, listening with half an ear as the engineer went through the same basic spiel presented by the other firms they'd heard. The fundamental problem was simple—Oakdale was growing too rapidly. More industries and private dwellings were being built than existing city services could handle. This Waste Management Committee was appointed by the mayor to look into alternatives and report their findings to the City Council. Kevin smiled secretly at the euphemism "waste management." Nobody wanted to talk about sewers or serve on a sewer committee. "We are, therefore, proposing a split treatment approach." Kevin tuned in fully at that statement. "One, to build a totally new waste treatment plant on Moore Creek; and two, to subsequently upgrade the existing plant."

Kevin cocked an intent ear. This was a twist he hadn't heard before. In general Kevin wasn't popular at these meetings because he supported what seemed to him a simple solution. Put a moratorium on all construction until the city could catch up with services. Gordon liked to have him sit in, though, to "keep the consultants honest," as he phrased it. Kevin glanced at Gordon, who raised an eyebrow in reply.

"Mr. Kendall," Kevin said, "what is your reasoning behind a split treatment approach? The city has already killed one stream with effluent. Why kill another?"

"Well, sir, the old treatment plant is obsolete. We see no way to close it down while a new one is being built on the same site. Cost-effectiveness would dictate building on a new site, then upgrading the old plant as monies become available. In that way it would be ready in future years to handle the additional growth this area will enjoy."

Kevin frowned at his choice of "enjoy" to describe the effects of growth. "What exactly are we talking about in terms of cost for your split approach, Mr. Kendall?"

Kendall shrugged. "You're looking at the twenty-five-million-dollar ballpark, either way you go at it. If we get started this year, we can probably get fifty percent federal financing. If so, we project no more than a one hundred percent increase in residential sewer bills over the next five years."

"What about industrial sewer rates?" Kevin pressed.

One of the businessmen on the committee turned, frowning. "Kevin, you know that some of our industries are currently paying thousands of dollars a month to the city for waste treatment. We can't possibly raise their rates as much as residential rates, or they would pick up and move out on us."

"Then our problem would be solved anyway, wouldn't it?" Kevin couldn't resist saying. "It seems to me it would be cheaper for the city and the residential customers to require some of the heavy industrial users to build pretreatment facilities."

Several committee members shook their heads. "Too expensive. Industries wouldn't stand for it."

"Kevin, you know what a hardship it's been on some of our plants since the state made us stiffen our standards," the chairman pointed out. "They're having to pay enormous fees to have some wastes hauled off. If we propose pretreatment to them, they'll move to Mexico or someplace and take all our jobs with them."

"They may not be paying as much to haulers as we think," Kevin replied. "I talked to a woman today who thinks someone dumped some toxic waste near her farm and killed her fish."

"I can't believe anyone in this community would do a thing like that," the chairman sputtered. "Thanks for coming, Mr. Kendall. We'll be taking this to the City Council in the very near future."

After the meeting adjourned, Kevin sat doodling as the room cleared, thinking these people couldn't see the forest for the trees. All they could think about was growth. New industries, more houses, and never a thought to the consequences on the bottom line. His anger at their shortsighted insensitivity was compounded by the sure knowledge that similar groups were making similar mistakes all over the face of the poor, old, battered globe.

"Do you feel as if you're talking to yourself?" Gordon grinned as he sat on the edge of the table near Kevin. "To most of these people, if one factory is good, then fifty must be fifty times as good. They sure don't make my job easy. Our back is to the wall, and they refuse to admit it. The new director of the State Pollution Control Agency is coming up next Friday to meet with us, and I suspect what this committee is going to hear is to get off their collective duffs or face a moratorium on any new construction."

Kevin looked surprised. "You really think so? The state has been waltzing around for two years making threatening noises, but nothing ever happens."

"New governor and new administration, my boy. From what I hear, they intend to light a fire under cities like ours, so it should be an interesting meeting." Gordon grinned again. "Put it on your calendar."

"I wouldn't miss it. They sound like my kind of folk."

Kevin walked out with Gordon, encouraged that someone might finally force Oakdale to face the need for responsible action about their burgeoning waste problem. When they reached the hall, he looked at his watch and waved farewell to Gordon. Time to keep his appointment with Becky Sherman, who was, beyond question, infinitely more interesting than waste management.

Sheila met Becky at the kitchen door. "Some guy from the State Pollution Agency called. Said he's sending someone out this afternoon to talk with you about the kill."

"Okay," Becky said, less than optimistic about what good it would do. "How are you getting along, Sheila?"

"No problem," her friend reported. "All hands are on deck and we're sailing right along. More to the point, how was your trip to city hall?"

"A possibly up ending to a definitely down day," Becky said. "Don't take that to mean my opinion of bureaucracy in general has changed," she cautioned Sheila, "because it hasn't. The only positive response I got was from an engineer at the city, and it has nothing to do with his work there. He's interested because he's studying biology at the university. That's the closest I could come to finding my tax money at work on my behalf."

"Maybe that's close enough. This situation probably needs some bright, young zealot not yet battered enough to know what he can't accomplish through the system."

"Well, he isn't that young, but he does seem to be bright, and he did listen to me all the way through, ask a few questions, and agree to come out this afternoon, so I can't complain about him. A slim hope is better than none, I always say. Now, what do I need to do for tonight, Sheila?"

"I hate to tell you, but you are totally dispensable here, Becky. Go tell your folks what's going on. Mondays are slow anyway, so I can't foresee anything I can't handle," she finished briskly.

"Monday or any day." Becky smiled at her thoroughly competent friend. "What would I do without you?"

"Lord only knows." Sheila rolled her eyes upward in a gesture of dismissal as she headed back to the kitchen. "See you whenever."

Becky left the restaurant and walked the hundred-plus yards to her parents' home, thinking how lucky she was to have Sheila on her team. When Becky came home and told her childhood chum about wanting to open Rainbow's End, Sheila's brown eyes glowed as she offered to work for practically nothing until they could turn a profit and it had been "they" ever since. Sheila proved to have a real talent for the business, quickly mastering each phase of the operation. She was as capable as Becky of doing everything from cooking to management of people and supplies. With any luck Rainbow's End would help Sheila put her daughter through college, and Becky was proud of that.

Becky was turning down the path to her parents' house when the county car pulled up beside her and a middle-aged man leaned out of the car window. "I'm looking for Becky Sherman. I'm from the County Health Department, and the State Pollution Control Agency asked me to come take samples of water and fish to send to their lab."

"I'm Becky Sherman. Drive down that way to the ponds. The samples I took Sunday are in the hatchery building."

The man smiled condescendingly. "I'm sorry, but I'll have to take my own samples. Do you want to ride down with me?"

Becky frowned as she reluctantly got into the car. "Why can't you take my samples? The kill was Saturday night, and I don't think you're going to find anything still hanging around."

He shrugged as he headed back down the driveway toward the ponds. "Probably not, but you have to understand our policies. We can only analyze samples we take ourselves. That keeps us from getting in the middle if somebody brings us doctored samples to get a neighbor or some industry in trouble."

"I resent the implication contained in that policy," Becky said tightly as they pulled up beside the hatchery building. "I scarcely think any business person would deliberately poison five thousand dollars' worth of his own fish for spite, do you?" She quickly exited the car, slamming the door with more force than was required to close it.

"I am in no way implying you would do that, Miss Sherman," he replied calmly. "I am simply stating our policy and the rationale behind it. Please be assured we will do the best we can to find the source of whatever problem you may have here." He took a lab kit out of the back seat of the car and walked toward the pond.

"The problem we have here is that some unknown person or persons in some way caused the death of a great number of our fish," Becky said sarcastically. "Shall I get one of the fish I kept from Sunday for you?"

The man packed up his water samples. "Sorry, same rule applies. I need to take one from the pond."

Becky stared at him uncomprehendingly. "You want a live fish from the pond? What can you tell from a live fish about what killed the others? If there's anything to be found, it seems to me it would be found in the fish that were killed by whatever it was."

He sighed patiently. "If heavy metal or something like that is involved, the lab might be able to find traces in the live fish. Some substance might be building up to a lethal dose in increments."

"Right, that's why a whole pond full of healthy fish suddenly start gasping for oxygen," Becky remarked disdainfully as she went for a dip net. "Have you a size preference?"

"The larger the better, I suppose."

Becky dipped a serving-sized trout out of the pond and put it into the man's extended plastic bag. "I'm sure Pollution Control will be back in touch with you, Miss Sherman. Thanks for your cooperation." He seemed anxious to be gone.

"Sure, any time," she said with a wry wave of her hand as she turned away, struggling to contain her anger. This was turning into a real education for Becky. She'd had no occasion to deal with local or state level public officials or agencies, assuming like most citizens they would be there if she ever needed them to protect her rights or interests. She was finding a far different ball game from the Washington scene she'd known so well. Then and there she decided to remedy that particular gap in her political education, being neither fond of nor accustomed to the role of helpless victim.

Becky entered the hatchery building to find her father bending over one of the tanks, silently watching the thousands of newly hatched trout called prefeeding fry. At this stage they simply lay on the bottom of the tank, living off the yolk still attached to them, unable to feed or swim. Gene was removing the few dead ones discernible by their white color.

"Hi, Dad," she greeted him. "A guy from the health department was just here to take samples for Pollution Control. Guess I'll throw away the samples I took. He says they could be faked, so he can't use them."

Gene looked up, a smile crinkling his weathered face. "Disappointed? You've got a lot to learn about the way government works, sugar. Don't get too upset over it though. No sense worrying about something we can't change."

"I can't help being upset, and I don't understand how you can be so calm about the whole thing," Becky sputtered. "In one fell swoop someone or something killed a great portion of the fish you'd raised from this size to grown. Don't you think somebody ought to pay for that?"

"Yes, baby, I do, but what I think ought to happen is probably a far cry from the reality of what will happen.

Chances are good we'll never even know what caused it." He shrugged, turning back to the tank.

"How can you say that so soon? There are all kinds of sophisticated tests for everything now," she insisted, more on hope than solid information. "Somebody should be able to trace it down for us."

Gene moved to the next tank. "Becky, you haven't heard some of the horror stories we hear at trout conventions. You don't know what you're up against. Sometimes it takes years to pinpoint the source of the kill. Sometimes they never find it or find it too late to recover damages from the polluter. I don't like to be cynical, but I'm telling you not to get too excited about Pollution Control sending you firm answers by return mail. I don't think that's very likely to happen."

Becky absently retrieved two dead fish from the tank in front of her. "Well, if they don't, we'll find someone who will," she said stubbornly. "I'm not putting all our eggs in one tank. A fellow from the city is coming out this afternoon to see what he can do. He's with the biology department at the university and interested in pollution and fish. Maybe he can help."

"Maybe so, but I don't want you to get your hopes too high, honey." He winked at her. "You know how daddies always try to shield their children from disappointment."

"And you know how much good it generally does with children in their thirties," Becky quipped, heading for the door.

"I don't recall it ever did much good with you," Gene chuckled as his headstrong daughter went off like Don Quixote to tilt at yet another windmill.

Chapter Three

Walking back to the ponds, Becky wished she had access to the sort of innate tranquility that seemed Gene's birthright. As she walked to the edge of the pond, fish clustered near her, a swarming, living kaleidoscope. She knew they "heard" her coming through vibrations in the ground and expected food. When none was proffered, they went about their business of being beautiful and graceful. Since childhood, Becky had come to watch the trout at times of trouble and distress. They were never still, but they were serenity in motion. They moved to live, to maintain the high oxygen level that ensured their survival, but their motion was smooth and purposeful, never frantic or erratic unless something was terribly wrong in their world. Her mind submerged to join the speckled bodies skimming along the bottom, to swim through the clear, cool environment where life was simple.

"Beautiful, aren't they?" Kevin's footsteps hadn't alerted even the trout, much less Becky, as he approached. She started at the sound of his deep, gentle voice above her.

'I've always thought so,'' she replied, getting to her feet. "Thanks for coming. Did you have any trouble finding us?''

"Not a bit, between my map and your signs." He grinned.

"What do we need to do first, Mr. McClain?''

"You need to call me Kevin, for starters." He grinned again, looking the bemused leprechaun. "Fish folk don't go in much for formality, Becky.''

"True," she agreed, "but I wasn't sure about city hall folk." Her tone was as light as his.

"Boy, you know how to hurt a guy, don't you? I'd rather you think of me as a fish folk, okay? Now, you said you took some samples Sunday. Do you still have them?''

"Yes, indeed." She smiled ruefully. "I offered them to the man from the health department who came to take samples for Pollution Control, but he didn't want them. Said we could have doctored them to incriminate some poor innocent industry we have it in for.''

Kevin chuckled, a warm bubbling sound that Becky enjoyed hearing. "I'm not hampered by his reservations or his policies, so I'll take them. Mostly, though, I want to just look around and ask a lot of questions. You do know this is basically a matter of detective work without the excitement you find in fiction. We search and search, hoping we find the right clues to lead to something significant. It's basically a process of elimination, slow but most likely to produce accurate results.''

Becky smiled. "I'm not much on calm and deliberate, but I have a father who is your kind of people,

Kevin. He'll be the one to answer questions, anyway. He's run this farm for thirty years . . . most of it without my interference, I might add."

"Let's walk the pond perimeters first so I can get my bearings, then we'll talk to your father," he suggested, setting off at a sturdy stride. As they walked, he stopped at intervals to pick up a twig or weed, study it briefly, and toss it down again. Becky tried to keep up with him and his many questions. "These ponds are fed by a spring, but are there any creeks or rivers nearby?"

"There's a creek on the other side of the hill," Becky replied, "but it's pretty small and not connected to us anywhere."

"Any chicken houses, hog operations, feedlots, anything like that nearby or above your spring?"

"No. There aren't even many cattle or any kind of livestock in any numbers."

He walked in silence, stroking his beard. "I'm sure you know what kills trout is usually not the pollutant itself, except in a very few cases of toxic chemicals. The fish suffocate because some substance ties up the oxygen in the water. Organic matter does that, sewage especially, and that makes it really tough to pinpoint a cause. Or it could be some sort of petroleum product that lies on the top of the water, preventing oxygen from mixing with the water, kind of like putting a garment bag over your head. Either way, by the time the fish die from lack of oxygen in the water, whatever tied up the oxygen has generally gone on downstream, and nothing shows in the fish. I hope you were able to salvage some of them. If tests show no toxins, we'll know they asphyxiated. They'd be perfectly okay to eat.''

"That's what Dad said, so we froze a lot of them. What you're saying about causes doesn't sound very encouraging, though.'' Becky felt her only hope beginning to dwindle, and her face betrayed the change in her emotional state.

Noticing the crestfallen look reforming Becky's pretty features, Kevin stopped and faced her directly. "Becky, don't get discouraged yet. We just have to start a methodical search of all the possibilities, eliminating them one by one and hoping there will be one left over.''

"That could take years, couldn't it?''

"Nobody can predict that," he admitted, "but one thing is sure: We can't start any earlier than today, so let's get on it. Where are your samples?''

"In the hatchery,'' she answered, indicating the low block building, "along with my equally patient and methodical father I want you to meet.'' She managed a wry tone that elicited another of Kevin's charming chuckles. Becky found she looked forward to seeing his face crease into the grin that seemed to precede the chuckle by a heartbeat. Despite his caution to her, Becky wasn't convinced detective work with this man would be without excitement. He carried himself with an air of careless confidence that intrigued her in one involved in such an exacting science. She liked the easy swing to his walk, the humor lurking so near the edges of his eyes. Thus far, she very much liked this Kevin McClain fellow, and she suspected Gene would feel the same.

Gene still hovered over the hatching tanks. He looked up as the screen door swung shut behind Becky and Kevin. "Dad, this is Kevin McClain," Becky introduced her companion. "Kevin, my father, Gene Sherman."

Within moments the two men were hunched over a tank deep in conversation about trout culture. Becky smiled and left to get the fish samples out of the processing shed refrigerator. Equally ignored, Major trailed her on her errand, waiting patiently outside the door where he knew he wasn't allowed.

Gene and Kevin met her near the fingerling tanks, still conducting a lively exchange, largely oblivious to their immediate surroundings, including Becky and Major. She was amazed at the level of animation between the two similarly calm, methodical, pragmatic people approaching her. She knew how Gene's face could light up when he talked about trout, but Kevin's demeanor was a mirror of that fascination. Becky felt even more certain she had found an ally in the search she had undertaken. Kevin's scientific patience, motivated by interest vital enough to send him back to the university at his age, could be critical before it was over, either solved or declared unsolvable by good authority.

"Beck, the least you can do for this helpful young man is to take him up the hill and feed him a good meal," Gene suggested amiably, his hand resting lightly on Kevin's shoulder. "After all, we want him to come back, don't we?"

"You bet," Becky said fervently. "Sheila should be just about ready to open the doors. Come on, Kevin."

Kevin looked down at his faded jeans and scuffed boots. "Uh, maybe I'd better take a rain check. I'm not really dressed for a place as fancy as I hear yours is."

Becky laughed, looking at her own casual clothing. "We're pretty nearly a matched set, Kevin, but I have an in with the management. Really, if you don't want to mix with the crowd, we'll sit at my table near the kitchen, but I would like you to eat with us. That's a pretty small price for the average professional consultant, isn't it?"

"Well, since you put it that way...." Kevin assented with a shrug. "Are you sure I won't drive down your property values?"

"If we can survive a fish kill, we can surely survive you," Gene laughed. "Go on now. I'll see you both later."

They walked up the steep path to Rainbow's End, arriving at the front door just as Sheila unlocked it. "Sheila, my dear, we have a hungry consultant here," Becky explained airily in response to Sheila's quizzical look. She introduced them over her shoulder as she headed for the kitchen. "Kevin, we serve the freshest, finest trout in every possible shape from plain charcoal broiled to drenched in fancy wine sauces. What'll you have?"

"Charcoal broiled sounds delicious, thanks."

"Good choice," she said briskly. "Sheila, he'll have two charcoal broiled. He only had an apple for lunch."

Sheila raised an eyebrow and smiled at Kevin, who looked astonished at Becky's statement. "Well, I never eat much for lunch," he stammered.

"What about you?" Sheila asked Becky.

"Traitorous as it may seem, I can't face a trout on a plate tonight." Becky shook her head woefully. "Just bring me a big salad or something, Sheila."

"You can't keep up your strength on salads," Sheila chided her boss, "and I'll bet you didn't have even an apple for lunch, did you?" When Becky hung her head guiltily, Sheila said, "That's what I thought. I'll surprise you," and walked toward the kitchen, her short blond hair gleaming in the flickering light from the ceiling lamps. Becky noticed Sheila was wearing one of their hostess gowns in spite of Becky's earlier assurances she would be back in time to take those chores. She chuckled, thinking Sheila sometimes knew her better than Becky knew herself.

Kevin scanned the interior of the restaurant. "Very nice, Becky. Did you do it yourself?" The deep luster of the native-wood wainscot lent gravity to the lightness of the wallpaper with its tumbling water and towering trees. The tables varied in size and shape, but all were old, made of wood and covered with tablecloths in pale blues and greens. There was an air of fineness and understated elegance to the room, but it was comfortable, not intimidating.

"Pretty much," Becky replied with a smile. "I'm glad you like it. There's a whole lot of me in this place." She followed his eyes with pride toward the windows overlooking the ponds. "Go look at the view while I get us something to drink. What would you like?"

"A beer would be perfect," he said, going toward the window wall. The broad windows looked out over the valley, with just enough trees taken off the hillside to provide intriguing glimpses of the trout ponds below. A quick movement at the periphery of his range of vision caught Kevin's eye. He turned to see a gray squirrel hanging head-down from the eave of the house, surveying the scene before dropping onto a bird feeder suspended there. "I see you, too, have a squirrel-proof bird feeder." He grinned at Becky as she approached with two frosty mugs of beer.

"They're tuning up for showtime," Becky commented as the squirrel wrapped neatly around the roof and swung to the feeder. "The customers love to watch their antics while they wait for dinner. You're looking at a seasoned performer there. All the birds, squirrels, and such are used to having people a foot away, so long as the glass is there. We have hummingbird feeders there, too," she added, pointing to red plastic tubes full of red nectar water. "Never say we don't have a good floor show at Rainbow's End."

They drifted back to their table, sipping suds off the top of the cold beer. "I don't drink much beer, but yours looked so good I couldn't resist," Becky commented. "Good stuff on a hot summer day, isn't it?"

"I got rather partial to it in places where it was safer than the water," he chuckled. "The company avoided a lot of problems by keeping us in beer."

"What company?" Becky queried. "Tell me about yourself, Kevin. What are you doing in school at this point in your life?" Becky's mother would have chided her for nosing into Kevin's personal affairs, but she didn't know any other way of finding out more about this interesting man who looked at the world through those startling blue eyes.

Kevin laughed, a deep rich sound against the polished wood behind him. "You mean, what is someone my age doing in college?" He held up a hand at her quick denial. "Hey, it's okay. Believe me, it's a common question. At my age I should be comfortably settled in a career, counting years until retirement, right?"

"That would be quite a count," Becky observed. "You're a long way from retirement age, Kevin."

"Turned the big four-oh last birthday. Time to start a new life and a new career, I said to myself when I couldn't blow out all the candles on one breath. There are some things I want to do in this life, and I decided I'd better get at it." A twinge of what looked like pain passed over his face quickly.

"What were you in your previous incarnation?"

"A petroleum engineer."

Becky was surprised. "A born-again polluter?" she blurted without thinking. "I mean, oil companies don't exactly sponsor Save the Wildlife programs, do they?" she followed up quickly, regretting the snide retort. "I'm sure that's not universally true, either...my stereotypes are showing. Sorry," she said and smiled guiltily. "Still, I'd think that would be a pretty exciting personal career to abandon."

Kevin smiled sadly. "I thought so for the first fifteen years, too. Got to go to a lot of exotic places, see strange and wonderful things, make a lot of money." He took a long draw on his beer. "When you're a kid, globetrotting in a fast-lane industry like petro-chem seems like heaven. You wonder why they pay you so much to have so much fun. As I got older and wearier, I slowed down and began to notice things I hadn't seen before, and I found I had a lot of trouble accommodating them. Believe me, your stereotypes aren't as far from the truth as I once wanted to think.'' He frowned, idly tracing the rim of his mug with one finger. ''There are things happening to the environment and to living creatures around this globe that would curl your hair, Becky.'' His eyes clouded as he seemed to distance himself from a painful thought. He tossed down the remainder of his beer, took a deep breath, and settled for a glib summary. ''By the time I hit forty, I knew I wanted to be part of the solutions, maybe in payment for being part of the problem for so long. So I simply chucked it all, stuck my passport in the bottom drawer, and enrolled in the unversity. As you said, born again.''

Becky was intrigued, less by what she heard than what she suspected he didn't say. Since it wasn't really any of her business, she merely asked, ''What are you going to do with a degree in biology?''

He shrugged. ''I'm not sure yet. A Ph.D. in microbiology has a lot of applications, but I'm especially interested in freshwater fish, protection of our streams and rivers and that sort of thing.''

''Well, I'd like to drink a toast to starting over,'' Becky proposed, raising her mug with a smile. ''It happens in the best of well-regulated lives.''

Kevin clinked his empty mug against hers. ''You, too?''

''Yep,'' she nodded emphatically. ''You see that dress Sheila is wearing? Well, I used to spend nearly every evening squeezed into one like that, going to parties and attempting to influence various political denizens of our nation's capital to protect funding for the arts and humanities. My official registration said 'lobbyist,' but don't be misled... I earned my living acting." She smiled wryly.

"Really? That sounds pretty exciting, too." Kevin leaned toward her, his chin resting on his hand, amusement in his eyes. "I've never known a professional lobbyist. Aren't they the people who buy politicians for clients like the oil company I worked for?"

"*Touché,* but this lobbyist happened to be pushing for a coalition of arts and humanities groups. Still, the life, and maybe the principle, is the same. Well, like you, I found it to be great fun for several years, full of bright lights and exciting, powerful people. And I always believed strongly in what I was doing; still do, for that matter. But the political climate has slowly cooled toward supporting the arts. I found myself increasingly unable to have the sort of impact I wanted to have." Absently, Becky rubbed the stone in her earrings, smiling ruefully. "Isn't that funny? I never stopped to think other people had stereotypes about lobbyists. I spent more time educating politicans than buying them... of course, our budget wasn't very good," she admitted with a smile.

"I expect you weren't any more typical of your profession than I was, but you will have to admit that lobbyists exercise a lot more influence for their employers than most voters realize or would approve of, for that matter. Maybe your cause was a little less environmentally damaging than mine, but, as you said, the principle is the same." He smiled, his point soundly home.

"Be that as it may," she acquiesced with a nod, "all that partying and hostessing, though, taught me a lot about this business, and when my folks built the new house and were trying to decide what to do with this old place, I had the bright idea of coming home to the Ozarks and turning it into a restaurant and club, which is, little by little, what we're doing."

"Is it turning out the way you thought it would?"

"So far, it's exceeded my modest expectations," she answered, her fingers crossed for luck. "At least until last Sunday, it had. We're finally beginning to make some money, but not enough to hold out long if we have any more problems or bad publicity growing out of it."

"Dreary conversation deadens even the most delicious food," Sheila chided as she set the plates of steaming food before them. "Idle chatter only, please."

"Yes, mother," Becky folded her hands obediently in her lap. "What's my surprise?"

"Chicken tarragon, and you will enjoy it," Sheila instructed with a shaking index finger under Becky's nose. "If you need anything else"—Sheila smiled pleasantly at Kevin—"she knows where to find it," she finished mischievously, moving quickly to greet a couple just entering the front door.

Kevin boned his trout with an efficiency seldom seen in a customer. Becky found most customers preferred having a waiter or waitress do it for them. "Hey, you're good. If the city ever lets you go, you can bone fish for me."

"There are days it would be a real relief," he said wryly. He lifted a fork of the flaky white trout to his mouth and leaned back, his eyes closed. "Superb," he pronounced heavenward before turning his blue eyes on Becky again. You're responsible for the idle chatter. I can see I will be much too busy to contribute.''

Becky always felt a glow when customers liked the food, but she was especially pleased by Kevin's approval. ''I'm really glad you like it. You will come back, then?''

''Every chance I get,'' he promised with a pixie leer. ''I'd like to think I'll have to make up excuses for coming back,'' he said, turning serious, his eyes blue arrows to her soul, ''but you and I both know there's a good chance of another fish kill.''

Becky's shoulders sagged. ''I was afraid you were going to say that.''

Kevin took a small notebook from his shirt pocket and wrote three phone numbers on it before tearing out the page. ''Here are the numbers where I can be reached day or night,'' he said as he handed Becky the paper. ''If it happens again, I want you to call me right away. We stand a lot better chance of pinpointing the source if we can get samples while the fish are dying. It doesn't matter when it happens, call me. Okay?''

''Okay,'' Becky sighed, tucking the numbers into her pocket, ''but I sure hope I don't need these numbers.''

They turned again to the food before them, making quick work of the delicacies. After coffee, Becky looked at Kevin solemnly, her wide, deep eyes troubled. ''Kevin, what do you think our chances really are?''

The blue eyes regarded her steadily. ''To be honest, the chances of another kill are good, much better than the chances of tracing what caused it. Tracking down something like that is a long, involved procedure, but I can promise you I'll give it my best.''

"I have a feeling your best is pretty good," Becky said with a smile, "so I'll take it."

"And more than welcome to it," he added in a soft voice, reaching out to squeeze her hand. "Thanks for a marvelous dinner, Becky. I'll pay you back one evening soon, if you'll allow me." He winked and made for the door with a wave of thanks to the passing Sheila.

Becky passed her friend at the foot of the stairs, her hand still warm from his touch. Sheila grinned and said, "He's a cute little devil, isn't he?" as Becky walked by.

For a moment Becky looked surprised. She was still thinking about Kevin's prediction of another kill. Her turquoise eyes studied Sheila's amused expression for an instant. "I guess he is at that," she agreed cheerfully. "At least one good thing has come out of all this, hasn't it?"

As she changed into a hostess gown to relieve Sheila, Becky called up the images of Kevin McClain stored in her memory banks. She studied the black hair and those startling blue eyes, wondering what ancestry produced such a striking combination of features. When she knew him better, she'd ask him about that. Most of all, she replayed the laughing eyes and the deep chuckle bubbling like a bottomless spring. Becky wanted to know Kevin McClain much better, to warm herself by the warmth he generated. She was more than a little curious about the emotional truth of his factual recitation concerning his decision to take an abrupt turn off the hitherto arrow-straight road of his life. She placed the scrap of paper carefully under her bedside phone. She might want those numbers even if there

were no more fish kills. Kevin McClain, the man, was
very appealing to Becky. He was sunshine and shadow,
the easy, surface accessibility a veneer for the deeper
and possibly darker recesses she suspected were there.
Becky realized she would like to explore all of that. For
years no man had so tantalized her, and she relished
the feeling, humming a happy little tune as she finished
dressing and went downstairs to work.

Kevin chuckled to himself as he drove back to his
apartment. He never would have looked at that lady
and figured her for a lobbyist. Beyond question, she
was beautiful enough to capture anyone's ear, but she
seemed far too straight-up and, well, real for his concept of the Washington lobbying circuit. It reinforced
his suspicion that Becky Sherman was a gem of many
facets, one he would like to subject to closer scrutiny.
He couldn't believe his good fortune. A puzzle that
would challenge his professional capacities and a woman who engaged his personal curiosity. Kevin grinned
widely, his sudden feeling of invigoration coming not
from the summer breeze flowing over his face but
from the unexpected windfall he knew would soon
fully absorb his attention.

Chapter Four

By Thursday, Becky had settled back into her regular routine. The sharp edges were gone from the memory of the fish kill until the phone rang midafternoon, and she found herself talking with an inspector from State Pollution Control.

"Ms Sherman? I'm calling to report back on the samples our lab received Tuesday morning. We found nothing in either the water samples or in the fish to identify any substance responsible for your kill."

Even though she hadn't expected anything more, Becky felt a twinge of disappointment tug at her for attention.

The voice continued. "With nothing more to go on, we can say only that some unknown transient substance apparently caused death by asphyxiation. Have you experienced this sort of thing before?"

"Never. Not in thirty years at this trout farm."

"Any obvious pollution sources nearby?"

"No."

"Well, if it hasn't happened before in thirty years,

it's probably a one-time accident of some sort. Let's hope it doesn't happen again."

Was hope the best he had to offer? "But what if it does? What then?"

"Give us another call and we'll be happy to check it out for you."

"Unless it happens between five on Friday and nine on Monday," she said, her voice heavily sarcastic.

The reply was measured and polite. "Ms Sherman, I'm sorry we weren't able to help you. We do the best we can with the resources we have, and they barely cover Monday through Friday."

"Right. Well, thanks for the call," she sighed, hanging up the phone. Somehow she wasn't comforted by his hoping it wouldn't happen again. Maybe Kevin had something by now on the other samples. She quickly dialed his office at city hall. "Kevin? Becky."

"Hi, Becky." The warmth of his voice caressed her ear. "What's up?"

"The state just called to say they didn't find anything in the samples they tested."

"Hmmm. Well, that doesn't really surprise me," he commented evenly. "Our lab should be through by this afternoon with the samples I took in. I'll pick them up and run out with them, if that's okay."

"That's great, Kevin," Becky said brightly. "Thanks."

"Maybe we could go to dinner," Kevin offered hopefully.

"Got to work tonight, but thanks anyway, Kevin. See you." Hanging up the phone, Becky thought how good she felt after talking with Kevin. Even when the news wasn't good news, his delivery made it more bearable somehow.

Becky busied herself with getting everything ready for the dinner crowd at the restaurant. Gene brought fresh fish up for the evening. They prided themselves on serving fish never more than a few hours from the pond. "Dad, the state called. Nothing showed up in the samples they tested."

"Didn't figure it would, did we?" Gene drawled.

"Kevin says he should have results on his samples late this afternoon. He's going to bring them out."

"That's a nice young fellow," Gene commented approvingly. "Knows a lot about fish, too."

Becky smiled, knowing Gene would consider Bonnie and Clyde "nice" if they knew a lot about fish. Still, he did take to Kevin faster than he usually did with strangers. Becky thought her dad was basically a pretty good judge of people, especially if one compensated for his possibly too-trusting nature.

They had just finished preparing all the fish for cooking when Sheila and Kevin came in together. "Look whom I found wandering around looking for an unlocked door." Sheila giggled. "Didn't you tell him about the servants' entrance?"

"Sorry, Kevin," Becky laughed. "The back door is always open."

"I'll remember that." He grinned, waggling his eyebrows at Becky. "Till how late?"

"Well, almost always open," she amended, her cheeks flushed at his subtle message, "for as late as it needs to be." She rolled her eyes upward. "Forget it. Tell me about the test results."

"The tests were all negative," he reported bluntly. "Whatever was there did its damage and moved on before you got the samples. No trace of toxins in the fish. They simply suffocated."

"That means it could have been anything," Gene said slowly, "which means we'll probably never know what it was."

Kevin nodded reluctantly, watching Becky's face.

"So what do we do now?" she queried with a sigh.

Stroking his beard thoughtfully, Kevin chose his words carefully. "We wait...." He didn't need to finish the sentence for anyone in the kitchen. Wait until it happens again.

Sheila spoke first, her vibrant voice breaking the gloom. "Becky, I've taken the liberty of making a date for you tonight."

Becky looked at her friend in disbelief. "You've what?"

"Dinner date," Sheila stated flatly. "I decided you needed a break tonight, so be on your way."

"What are you talking about?" Becky frowned in confusion.

"She's talking about me," Kevin admitted sheepishly. "I figured I'd get further through Sheila."

"If we get busy tonight, Sheila will need...."

"I think Frances and I can handle any emergency Sheila has." Gene grinned at his daughter. "Have a good time."

"No fair pulling rank," Becky threw at Gene. "What an uppity bunch of hired help I have here!" She was more pleased at the prospect of a night off, especially with Kevin, than she was at Sheila's obvious attempts to play cupid with her, but she knew when she was outnumbered.

Kevin winked at Sheila and steered Becky toward the door. "Everyone should have such help."

Conflicting feelings of excitement and guilt gripped Becky about taking a night off in the middle of the week. She had been at the restaurant every night it was open for more than two years. Before that, she only missed when she was sick. She'd certainly never played hooky to go to dinner with a man. Come to think of it, she had trouble remembering the last real date she'd had.

"Hey, nobody is indispensable, boss lady. Sheila seems quite competent," he remarked wryly as if he read Becky's thoughts. "Where would you like to eat?"

"Anywhere, so long as it's fattening junk food."

Kevin laughed. "Well, I must admit I had in mind something a little more exotic and romantic, but if the lady wants junk food, I know just the place." He drove straight to the nearest pizza parlor and ordered a supreme with everything. After they finished off the pizza, Becky allowed she still had room for an ice-cream cone, so the next stop was the ice-cream shop.

Becky felt lighthearted in a way she hadn't for years. They talked about everything and nothing, licked their ice-cream cones fast enough to keep them from melting, stopped by the park to swing a while and watch the moonlight on the backs of the sleeping ducks around the pond. When at last Kevin parked beside the restaurant, both were reluctant to let the evening end.

"Surely there's some beautiful overlook handy,"

Kevin suggested hopefully as they got out of the car. "Isn't there?"

"Of course," Becky assured him, taking his hand and leading him down the path to a boulder on the hillside just above the huge spring noisily cascading life into the trout ponds. The moon rippled in her field of dark mirrors, and the night vibrated with the nocturnal communion of unseen insects. Early summer was Becky's favorite time on the farm, with the possible exception of dogwood time when the still bare woods were sprinkled with the starkly white promise of spring. She perched tailor-fashion on the big rock. "How's this?" She smiled at the shadowy Kevin.

He leaned against the rock, his arm resting easily against Becky's leg. "It unquestionably qualifies as a beautiful overlook," he confirmed. "I can see I've missed a lot of treasures hidden in these hills, including you," he said softly. Impulsively, his lips brushed her cheek.

The teasing quality of Becky's voice hid the pleasure she felt at his nearness. "I was only hidden from you because you eat at the wrong places."

Kevin chuckled. "I ate at so many classy joints in my former life, I vowed when I came here I would never again wear a suit and tie for the privilege of eating a meal...or for much else, if the truth be known." He hitched himself onto the rock to sit beside her. "However, after seeing what some classy joints have to offer, I may have to reconsider my decision."

Becky giggled. "Not on my account. I dress up for work, but it's a uniform. You can sit at my table in whatever you're wearing, Kevin."

He slipped his arm around her waist and pulled her to him. "Do you have any idea how much I've enjoyed your company this evening, Becky?"

"Couldn't be as much as I have enjoyed the evening," she said, snuggling against him. "I can't remember the last time I sat out here and just drank up the beauty of this place." Her normally husky voice softened toward a whisper. "Never on a work night, and never with better company, Kevin."

He brushed a kiss on her cheek. "Well, since we seem to be in agreement, it behooves us to do it again as soon as possible, wouldn't you say?"

Becky returned kiss for kiss, giggling at the feel of his beard against her lips. "I'd certainly say so. Sunday is my official night off."

"Seems like a long time from now, but would you care to sign up for another junk food junket Sunday night?"

She laughed merrily. "My stomach has a limited tolerance for pizza, but a limitless appetite for good food, so I'd love to have you as a partner in crime to sample the other culinary delicacies of every corner of the globe." She smacked her lips theatrically. "Yumyum: nachos supremo, langostini and pasta, bushels of boiled shrimp, sweet and sour everything... well, everything but trout...."

"I'll have to schedule time for an extra five miles of jogging every Monday"—he laughed genially—"but it'll be worth it."

"And I'll have the pot at Rainbow's End," she punned, patting her flat belly.

"Oh Lord," Kevin groaned. "Bad joke. If that's

what a night off does to you, maybe I should reconsider my offer."

"No way, Jose," she snickered, her hand turning his face toward her. "You're good for me," she whispered as she kissed him lightly.

"That was a nice sample," he murmured, "but I'd like something more to take home with me." Gently, tenderly, he captured her lips in a warm bonding. Becky pressed against him, responding to his warmth like a lazy cat at a fireplace. "Do I have to leave the rest for another night?" he husked as he drew away.

Becky pulled from his grasp and stood. "Whew, you're moving a little fast for me, Kevin."

"Can I help it if you inspire my adrenaline?" He grinned disarmingly, getting up with a leap. "Listen, I'll walk you back to the restaurant, Becky; then I have to get on home, much as it pains me to say it. Tomorrow is a school day, you know." He shook a parental finger under her nose.

"I handle happiness better in small doses, too," Becky said, squeezing his hand as they walked back up the hillside. "At least until I've built up a reasonable tolerance level again."

"Hey, lady, don't look now, but I think we've got something going here," he said, and grinned broadly as they reached the back door, "and I, for one, couldn't be more delighted to have found this pot of gold... with nary a leprechaun to help me."

"Why would you need one?" Becky giggled. "I think you are one, Mr. McClain. A little oversized, maybe, but definitely of the same devious and pixilated breed, I'd say. Take your pixie dust and go. There'll be another night."

"Sweet dreams, colleen," he teased, kissing her gently before swinging off toward his car, whistling a jolly little jig tune as he went.

Her face flushed and smiling, Becky slipped through the back door to be immediately noticed by Gene and Sheila, who looked at her and at each other. "Nothing like a night off to fix you right up," Gene said and winked at Sheila.

"If that's what it does to you, I'd like to put in my request for one." Sheila grinned mischievously. She pushed Becky toward the kitchen door. "Get your money's worth out of it. Go on up and luxuriate in the glow. We have everything under control here, haven't we, Gene?"

"Looks that way to me, Sheila," he agreed, folding his arms over his chest.

Becky's laugh filled the air with specks of light. How could anybody be lucky enough to have Gene, Sheila, and now Kevin in her corner? "With an act like that, you two should go on the road. Sherman and Marlowe, matchmakers par excellence."

"Enjoy it while you can," Sheila cautioned. "I expect to see you down here in your glad rags tomorrow night. I'm out of clean shawls."

The ripples of laughter from the conspirators followed Becky up the stairs to her apartment. She could hardly believe everyone had taken to Kevin so quickly, including herself. There was an easy familiarity between Kevin and her that usually came only with much longer association. Wouldn't it be fun to have someone like Kevin to be with, to share things with, to get to know, to experience the kind of feelings she held close as she slipped into her bed? Becky devoutly hoped it

wasn't just pixie dust in her eyes, that the potential between them was as vital and real as she felt at this moment it might be. With Rainbow's End getting on its
feet, she was ready for a new challenge, and she was
wise enough to know human relationships are at the
top of that category. Still, Becky reminded herself, she
had to go at her own rate. She had tried letting someone else set the pace, but it never worked for her. If it
felt too fast, it probably was too fast, at least for her,
and she'd learned to pay attention to her feelings about
herself in relation to men. She drifted into a drowsy
reverie, comforting herself with how slowly some birds
seemed to fly but how very high they seemed to soar by
doing it their own way.

A little late arriving at the conference room, Kevin was
surprised to note not only the regular members of the
Waste Management Committee in attendance, but the
mayor and several members of the City Council. Several strangers sat at the head table, no doubt the state
folk the mayor wanted to impress. Kevin took a seat
near the back just as the mayor called the meeting to
order.

"Today, we're very happy to have with us the new
Director of the State Pollution Control Agency, Mrs.
Janice Miller." A smattering of polite applause greeted
the tall, middle-aged woman rising from her seat at the
table. Her demeanor struck Kevin as low-keyed professional, consistently underrated at the opposition's peril.
She had warm dark skin, gleaming hair pulled into a
soft chignon, and piercing ebony eyes that scanned the
assembly before she spoke.

"Ladies and gentlemen, I am happy to be here on behalf of Governor Ray and the agency I head up. As you know, the governor is vitally interested in environmental affairs and anxious to assist cities and counties in bringing their waste treatment programs into compliance with federal and state standards. We've been busy reviewing all the records in our office and making changes necessary to implement this new philosophy." She smiled and looked around the room, sizing up her audience's attitudes. "I am here today to try to help you bring your waste treatment procedures and facilities into compliance."

Several people shifted uneasily in their chairs as Mrs. Miller continued. "Our records show Oakdale was ordered two years ago to begin seeking remedies for the amount and quality of effluent it was putting into the river below the treatment plant. You were given deadlines to submit certain plans and timetables to my office, but those documents were never forthcoming. When I took office six months ago, I notified you that a plan for dealing with this problem must be on my desk within one hundred twenty days, including an increase in standards for industrial effluent." Her smile was not benign. "As of this date, I have no evidence of your having even considered this problem seriously, let alone dealt with it."

Kevin could see the agitation rippling through the group as Mrs. Miller's onyx eyes fastened on the mayor, who began sputtering excuses. "Well now, Mrs. Miller, that's not quite an accurate portrayal of our efforts. We've had a number of engineering firms working on the problem, and we have raised the industrial standards, much to the detriment of our local industries, I might add. These things take both time and money, which is always in short supply."

Kevin enjoyed the mayor's discomfort. His amusement was enhanced by the directives coming from a woman Kevin knew most of the men in the room thought should never be in a position to tell them what to do.

"I realize you need time and money," Mrs. Miller acknowledged, "and we will help you with both. But let me make it perfectly clear that we expect things to proceed in a timely fashion. We will not extend the sort of benign neglect you enjoyed under the previous administration. After all, your first warning came two years ago, so you've been using up your allotment of time. We expect some sort of plan from you within thirty days."

The committee chairman gasped. "Ma'am, there's no way we can come up with a plan in that time. Can't we get another extension?"

"My office prefers giving technical assistance over giving extensions." She smiled coolly. "We will work with you and give you all the help we can, but we expect results. We have recently placed moratoriums on any new sewer connections in two cities in this state, which means no new industry and no new houses until the waste treatment plants are upgraded to handle it. I don't imagine you want that to happen to Oakdale." With a slight nod, she thanked them for their attention and walked out with Gordon, leaving a grinning Kevin amid a committee babbling about disaster wrought by new governors and uppity women.

Delighted as he was by Janice Miller's time bomb, Kevin knew further increases in industrial standards could mean an increase in incidents of dumping. Oakdale's back was to the wall now, and they would pass that pressure along. Becky Sherman might not be the last person to pay the price. For that matter, the chances were greater for another kill at Rainbow Ribbon. Kevin decided he'd better keep in close touch with Becky and the trout this weekend.

Becky checked out the last dinner guests and roped off the dining room, funneling traffic into the club area, open two hours longer than food service. Friday and Saturday nights a good little jazz combo held forth in the club, drawing in a number of music fans after the dinner hours. The front door opened to admit two of the regulars, followed by Kevin.

After acknowledging the customers, Becky turned to Kevin in surprise. "It's only Friday. I thought our junket wasn't until Sunday."

"It isn't, but I got lonesome." A grin split his face. He cocked his head toward the club. "Hey, they're pretty good. I didn't hear that last night."

"We can only afford them on weekend nights," Becky explained. "You bet your hat they're good. I handpicked them, and I sing with them once in a while, too."

"You sing, too?"

"Mostly for my own pleasure these days, but I once considered a singing career . . . that is, until I found out how little money is available to how many talented people. A lot of the people around here have been listening to me since I was a kid, and they're really disappointed when I don't perform at least once a week. I really love the kind of jazz we do; it sort of takes me out of the more mundane world of profit margins between leaf and head lettuce." She laughed. "Don't I look like a cabaret singer?"

Kevin looked at Becky as if seeing her for the first time. "Better than any I've seen lately. You look really terrific." His eyes roamed over the tomato-red gown she wore so well. A deep cleavage in the dress bared a considerable expanse of creamy-tanned skin, and the tiny remnant of bodice draped gracefully from the curve of her breasts into a small waist defined by a silken cord shot with silver. From there, the long skirt descended in clinging folds to silver strappy sandals.

Becky struck a theatrical pose. "Just your average working girl's uniform. Thanks for noticing."

"By my patron saint, I hope I never live so long as to fail noticing such a vision," he prayed fervently toward the ceiling.

Becky laughed, her spun-silver earrings scattering light. "Seriously, are you here to admire the fixtures, listen to the music, or what exactly?"

"All of the above," Kevin said with a grin. "I'll bet we can hear the music from the hillside, I've already expressed my admiration of the fixtures, and, to make a long story short, I thought we might go soak up some of this very pleasant evening. If you're needed, you'll be close by, but I'd really enjoy sitting on a quilt with you for a while."

"I'd love to, Kevin. I'll run upstairs and change out of the uniform first."

"I'll just stand here and sigh while I watch you run up the stairs," he said with a comic leer.

"Lord, don't make me self-conscious or I'll fall on my face." Becky chuckled as she started up the stairs. "I won't be long."

Kevin leaned his back against the wall, an enigmatic smile playing across his lips. He was glad Becky had accepted his presence at face value. While he spoke the truth in saying he wanted to be with her, and not only tonight, that wasn't all there was to it. He didn't want to unduly alarm Becky, but he was ninety percent sure someone was dumping illegally on the weekends. It was the usual pattern, and he felt sure this would be no exception. He wanted to be here when it happened, even though he wasn't totally sure what could be done other than taking samples and anything else that occurred to him at the moment. His hidden vigil would give him additional opportunity to get better acquainted with this extraordinarily appealing woman, something he wanted very much to do.

Becky's reappearance in cotton shorts and gauzy top interrupted his thoughts. "I'll bet you'd look good in a burlap bag," he commented appreciatively. "I have some wine in the car if you can come up with glasses."

"Glasses we have," she assured him, stepping over the chain into the dining room. She ducked into the kitchen, returning with two stemmed glasses. "Don't be intimidated by the expensive look. We buy them by the case."

Along with the wine, they retrieved a battered quilt and an oil lantern from Kevin's car and walked down the path to the overlook. "I like to see people's faces

when we talk," Kevin explained with a shrug when
Becky questioned him about the lamp. "I won't turn it
high enough to dilute the moonlight."

"Nut," she chuckled, preceding him to their destina-
tion. While he lighted his lamp, Becky spread the quilt
on the ground below the boulder. Kevin uncorked the
wine with his Swiss army knife and filled the glasses to
the rim.

"I'd like to propose a toast to choices—quilts over
party linen, the moon over city lights, and tomorrow
over yesterday," Kevin proposed loftily, clinking his
glass against Becky's.

"I will certainly drink to that," Becky echoed the
sentiment. "I've seen enough partying and city lights
to last me a lifetime. But I really came back because I
wanted to be here, not because I wanted to leave there.
Do you understand that, Kevin?"

"Indeed I do." He nodded emphatically. "There's a
vast difference between running away from something
and running toward something. I think I'm just making
that transition, Becky. At first I just wanted to get away
from my old life. Now I'm thinking about where I want
to go when I finish my degree, what I really want to do,
and with whom. I haven't done that until very lately."

Becky sipped the fruity cool wine. "I'm already
where I want to be. I'm at home here, I've never found
any place lovelier, I like what I'm doing. Not many
people have a life that good, Kevin. I honestly hadn't
given much thought to the whom part of my future for
a number of years."

"Why not, Becky?" His voice was quiet, his eyes
fixed on her face.

"Oh, I don t really know," she sighed, thinking over the years in Washington. "All my time went into trying to build my career, and a good relationship requires maintenance, which means time. Too, most of my business associates were politicians or other lobbyists, a notoriously transient lot."

"Like petroleum engineers?"

"I guess so, but the per capita ego quotient is probably a little steeper in political circles. Most of the men there seemed to operate in hyperdrive, sort of hit and run transient relationships, and the harder they pushed me, the slower I went until they passed me and went on. Anyway, you know how tough that sort of life can be." Memories flowed into Becky's mind. "It's a great life for a while, but it's for young people and fanatics. One day you wake up wondering what it's all about, where you're really getting to, working all day to gather ammunition for those new contacts, talking yourself blue in the face to people who think arts and humanities are trivial pursuits at best, if they ever think about it at all. When you can't stand another politician who is more interested in your cleavage than your cause, you realize you no longer fall in the fanatic category. If you're not among the young, it gets harder and harder to get yourself out there again and again. I was getting to the point where I couldn't face another single party when a cut in funding forced me to make a choice. I knew right then it was time for a change."

"But you've been back here for a number of years, haven't you?"

"Four," Becky stated, "but I've been pretty tied up trying to make a go of my new career. I haven't been looking for anyone, and if someone happened by, I figured I would notice and do something about it then." She drew another mouthful of the wine. "I'm pretty picky when it comes to men."

"Seems to me you have exquisite taste," he commented with a courtly nod of his head.

"Seems that way, doesn't it?" Becky smiled. "What about you? You can tell I've been away from the city for a while. I just assumed you weren't married or you wouldn't be here."

"In my case, that's a safe assumption." He lay back on the quilt, the lamplight glinting off the silver strands in his hair. "I was married early on, but all the moving around and being sent off to places where wives can't go tends to interfere with domestic tranquility." Becky thought she caught a taste of bitterness in his tone. "As you said, any relationship requires maintenance, and it doesn't work as well long distance for long periods of time. After five years, we agreed it just wasn't working out to be the best thing for either of us, so we split the blanket. She went her merry way and I went mine."

"Sorry," Becky murmured, thinking he didn't sound very merry.

"No reason to be," he replied shortly.

"What was she like?" Becky asked, not sure why she wanted to know, but knowing she wanted to ask.

"She was a really nice person who deserved better than I could give her and had the good sense not to settle for less."

"Judging from Sheila's experience, divorces must be pretty awful, even when it is the best thing for everybody," Becky offered sympathetically.

Kevin stared into the darkness for a long moment before answering in a carefully controlled voice. "It was pretty painful at the time, but I've come to terms with it and learned a lot from it, I think. I don't intend to make the same mistakes next time." Noticing the somber note in his voice, he quickly raised up for a swallow of wine. "Why make the same mistake twice when there are new ones waiting to be made?" he quipped cheerfully, having moved to a safe distance from that too-slowly fading pain.

"So here we are. An overaged college student and an underaged old maid, both trying to decide what to do with what's left of our lives," Becky summarized wryly. "I personally believe in taking life one step at a time. I think our next step should be to close the space between our lonesome bodies," she suggested in a husky voice full of warmth and vitality.

Kevin laughed, the delighted sound rumbling from his chest. "You silver-tongued devil," he said, reaching for her, "what a way you have with words. Now who's moving too fast?"

Becky rested on Kevin's broad chest, her head bent to his lips with the answer. He met her halfway, his soft mouth coaxing her to follow him into a sensory world Becky realized she had missed during her celibacy. The feeling of his strong hands on her back, his breathing beneath her, the contrasting softness of his lips and the harsher texture of his mustache and beard immersed her in a pool of sensations she savored. He was gentle and undemanding, enjoying the feel of her, yet she knew desire would build like a prairie fire when they were ready to face that complication. For tonight, it was enough to hold each other, to lie together, listening to the night sounds, talking softly and watching the lamp-light flicker over each other's forms. From Kevin's responses, Becky wondered how long he would be comfortable with her leisurely approach. For that matter, how long would she?

Saturday night's heavy business kept Becky too occupied to think about other problems. Still, she caught herself glancing expectantly at each new arrival, hoping Kevin would appear in the door. Even though their date was for Sunday, she rather thought ... or maybe just hoped ... he might show up unannounced. Becky admitted to herself that she really wanted to see him again, that she felt very good in his company.

As she ushered the last of the club's customers out and closed up, a damp pool of disappointment spread through her. She chided herself for being silly, but she couldn't comfort the part of her that missed seeing Kevin's animated face, a grin splitting his beard. She decided a short walk in some fresh midnight air would drain off some of the frustrated energy and help her to sleep. She slipped out the back door through the kitchen, trading her pumps for sneakers always kept by the back door for quick runs down the hillside.

Strolling slowly along the brow of the hill, idly scanning the silent trout ponds in the valley below, Becky took great gulps of the summer air. She stopped with a gasp directly above the spring, where the silver moon-light glanced off a dark shape she knew shouldn't be there. For a moment, she debated what to do if she were seeing what she thought she saw. Staring through the mottled darkness of the hillside, Becky assured herself that someone sat on a rock overlooking the spring, and she wanted to know who. She started down the hillside path, calling with what she hoped sounded like authority. "Who's there? This is private property, and you're trespassing."

The figure stood abruptly and turned to face her. A voice came up to meet her. "Becky? It's me, Kevin."

Involuntarily, her hand went to her chest in a gasp of relief. "My heavens, Kevin, you scared me to death. I thought some drunk had wandered down here and couldn't figure out where he was."

"You didn't sound scared," he said as she approached. "What are you doing out here this time of night?"

As she reached his side, the full realization struck her. "I live here, but I'd like to hear your answer to the same question." She frowned, thinking of the thwarted anticipation of the long evening. How long had he been here without letting her know? "You could at least have told me you were on the premises," she said, miffed at his silence.

"Becky," he started to explain, "I knew you were busy from all the cars in the lot, and I just . . . well, I thought I should keep an eye on things tonight."

"Keep an eye on what, and why couldn't you stop in to tell me what you were up to?" she demanded impatiently.

"I didn't want to worry you unnecessarily," he admitted, placing his hands on her arms lightly.

Becky shook off his hands. "That worries me even more," she snapped. "Kevin, I am not some airheaded child who needs protection from the truth or anything else much, and I don't appreciate your thinking I am. What is this terrifying truth you think I can't handle?" Fists on hips, she waited for an answer.

"Don't make so much of it, Becky," he said with a frown. "I just think there will be another kill, and I want to stay close, to be here if it happens."

"And why, all of a sudden, do you prefer your own company to mine?" she blurted out accusingly. "I have more interest in those fish than you do."

Kevin frowned in confusion. "Becky, you're talking as if I really am trespassing where I'm not wanted. What's the matter with you? After last night I thought...."

"After last night I thought a lot of things, too." She laughed shrilly. "I thought you were out here because you liked my company, not my fish; I thought you were substantially different from other men I have known; I thought a lot of things that may have been pretty far off base, I find." A turmoil of unwanted images muddied her usually sensible head.

"Just hold it right there," Kevin snapped with authority, the amiable lines of his face suddenly hard. "I got here tonight, saw the rushing business, figured you were busy. I came alone because of that and because I'm not all that sure I'm right about all this. I believe that one weekend soon, there will be another kill, but I didn't want to add to your worries with nothing more than a hunch." He grasped her hands firmly. "As for last night, I was here for both you and the fish. I was not just using you to pass the time, if that's what you're thinking."

Becky sagged, hoping he couldn't see how close he'd

come to his target. She'd never admit jumping to that conclusion, but she felt the doubt fading at his assault. "Kevin, I'll stop jumping to unwarranted conclusions if you'll stop assuming I need protection from reality."

"It's a deal," he said, squeezing her hands. He released one hand and tilted her chin to look into his eyes. "Becky, please don't ever think I would use you that way. It's not my style with anyone, least of all with you. Okay?"

She nodded, unsure what to say. "Shall I wait a while with you?"

"You don't have to. I took it easy today, knowing I planned to camp here tonight, but I know you're tired. Go get some sleep, huh?"

"No, really, I'm fine. I'd rather stay, at least for a little while. I've been looking for you all evening, Kevin," she admitted softly, "and I can't just say 'hi' and go off to bed so easily."

"I'm glad you found me," he whispered before kissing her slowly, warmly. "While you're here, would you like to spend all of tomorrow with me, doing something fun? Suddenly dinner just isn't enough of you to suit me."

"Something fun like what?" she asked, smiling from the shelter of his circling arms.

"Let's go to Eureka Springs," he improvised, thinking anything with Becky would be fun enough.

"Oh, that's one of my favorite places," she said in delight, "and I'd love to go there with you, Kevin."

"Good. Let's have lunch at Bit o' Sweden on the way. I'll pick you up about eleven?" He nuzzled her neck gently with his lips. "If I were just using you last night, would I be asking you for a real date?" he whispered.

She pushed him away, indignant until she saw the mischievous grin on his face. "I asked for that, didn't I?" She laughed. "Maybe you are substantially different from most of the men I've known in recent years. Give me a real kiss while I think about it."

He kissed her with enthusiasm and depth, but pulled away saying, "Now that we've settled that, go to bed. I'll call you if anything happens."

"Why can't I stay?"

"You can, but if you do, I'm leaving," he said patiently. "There is no point in both of us wearing ourselves out, much as I enjoy your company. We may be at this for some time, so it makes sense to me for us to split the watches."

"I detest irresistible logic," she grumped. "I agree only if each lonely watch is preceded by a short period of snuggling and storing up warmth against the night. Under those terms I agree to go away until tomorrow night."

"Well, maybe you could stay just a few more minutes." He smiled, reaching for her. "You could always drive tomorrow while I take a nap."

Eureka Springs, touted as the little Switzerland of the Ozarks, lay strewn over the mountains some fifty miles of steep and winding highway from Oakdale, its picturesque Victorian houses like carved beads along the single street stringing them around the mountain's neckline. They parked the car in a lot and waited for the little rubber-tired motor trolley to take them into the heart of town. The jovial driver assured them they had parked about as close as they could have, considering the crowd for the arts and crafts fair in progress.

Becky clasped her hands. "What luck, Kevin. I love to prowl these fairs, but I have to keep my hands in my pockets or I always buy too many things." Booths and shops along the steep, winding street lured them and other tourists into displays of pottery, quilts, jewelry, leatherwork, and all the other handmade items produced by the sizable colony of artists and craftspeople in the area. "Oh, look, Kevin. Have you ever seen such pretty things?" she bubbled, buzzing from one booth to the next, settling briefly before a table of jewelry of different designs and types, but having in common the same stone set in each. The setstones, ranging from a rosy dawn through a dusty mauve to nearly gray, swirled and streaked individualistically like abstract miniatures. "That's mozarkite," she explained to Kevin, "and it's native to the Ozarks. Isn't it lovely?" She tried on a ring, turned an oval brooch thoughtfully in one hand before her eye was caught by a small dusty rose stone set in a delicate silver filagree pendant and flanked by tiny, matching ear studs.

Kevin watched Becky's eyes light up as she reached to stroke the highly polished stone. "It looks like a piece of sunrise," he commented admiringly, knowing how exquisite it would look on her, "and I think it looks like you." Without further consultation, he handed it to the woman and wrote her a check for the set.

"Kevin, you really shouldn't . . . ."

"I'm old enough to do whatever I want to do, and I

want to do this," he interrupted cheerfully. "You do like it?"

"I love it, but...."

"Then my taste is as good as I thought it was." He grinned, handing her the box. "Let's go sip some spring water and you can put them on. I'll fasten the chain, but those earrings are beyond my skill," he admitted amiably.

They sat on the porch of a restaurant, sipping lemonade made with spring water, and Becky put on the jewelry. "They look much nicer on you than they would have on anyone else," he asserted firmly, "so I couldn't just leave them there, could I?"

Becky laughed happily. "Thank you so much, Kevin. They can keep me company on my watch tonight. I hope they bring me as much luck and happiness as you do."

Until nearly dark they strolled hand in hand through the picture-postcard town, admiring the recently restored residential areas, marveling at the challenge of building a town in the deep folds of the mountain's stony cloak. Kevin couldn't believe the nine-story hotel whose entire spinal column rested against a bluff. "Every floor a ground floor," he marveled. Checking his watch, Kevin reminded her of the last trolley run. "I think I'm about walked out. My calf muscles feel like I've climbed miles today, all uphill."

On the way out of town, they stopped at a hilltop restaurant for catfish and hush puppies, pronouncing the day an unqualified success. "I hope I don't go to sleep at my post," Becky giggled as they left. "I've had a lot of exercise today."

"I could stay with you," he offered quickly.

"Nope," she stopped him preemptively, "we agreed. I'll take a short nap while you drive home, and I'll be fine. It's my turn, and I'll take it."

Kevin followed the snaking road in the gathering darkness. "Put your head on my leg, and I'll drive carefully." They sped on toward home, the warm weight of Becky's head pressed against Kevin's body, his mind straining to concentrate on his driving.

Becky sat on the hillside, watching Kevin's car drive away, almost wishing she had let him stay longer. They'd had such a lovely day together, she thought, absently rubbing a finger over the smooth stone at her throat. She felt so alive, so laden with potential when they were together, but a serious relationship needed far more than that to go the distance. She sat, arms wrapped around her knees, thoughts wrapped first around Kevin, then around the defenseless fish below her, unaware of her vigilance. Kevin would have to take a back seat for a while, at least until she could divert some of her energy and time from the protection of her livelihood and her parents' life vested in the silent swimmers who depended on her.

Chapter Five

The cold clear eye of a full moon glinted off the pipe as Charley and Leo made the connection. Charley wished he'd come alone; Leo was like a cat on a hot tin roof, starting at every cricket chirp.

"Charley, it's only been two weeks," Leo whined nervously. "You told me this was just for emergencies, just once in while."

"Leo, the pond's overflowing. We got to do something with it, don't we? It didn't cause any trouble last time, did it? What are you so worried about anyway?" Charley's patience with the younger man was beginning to fray.

"Listen, Charley, somebody was telling my old lady a bunch of fish got killed at the trout farm a couple weeks back. Somebody they knew got a lot of trout for their freezer by helping clean some for Mr. Sherman. You don't reckon...."

"Oh, hell, Leo," Charley growled, "you know damn well this creek doesn't run into that trout farm."

"It runs on the other side of the hill," Leo protested.

"Well, now, how did it get over the hill, Leo? Walk?

Besides, I told you this stuff won't kill anything, didn't I?"

"Yeah, I know what you said, but Mr. Sherman's a real nice fellow, Charley. I used to work summers for him, and he always treated me real good. I went to school with his kids, Charley, and I sure wouldn't want...."

"Forget it, Leo." Seeing the frown on Leo's face, Charley took another tack. "That fancy restaurant out there is where the boss always takes the big shots when they're in town. You don't think he'd poison his own plate, do you?" he laughed.

"I sure would hate to think this would hurt the Shermans, Charley. It just wouldn't be right to do that."

"You worry too much, kid. Go see if it's all through the pipe yet."

As Leo walked down the brushy hillside to the hidden pipe, he worried, but he couldn't really see how anything could get from a creek clear through a mountain to the trout ponds. Maybe Charley was right. Maybe Leo just worried too much. But the more he thought about it, the harder it was not to worry.

Friday night was so busy Becky and Sheila were like shuttles on a busy freeway, barely finding time to exchange greetings and vital information. Sheila looked after a private anniversary party in the sunporch while Becky worked the main dining room. Each made occasional forays into the club and kitchen to be sure things were running smoothly. Near closing time, Sheila sailed by the register, stopping long enough to ask Becky if Kevin was expected.

"I couldn't say, Sheila. I haven't heard from him today."

"Be a shame to waste that full moon." Sheila winked as she continued toward the kitchen.

As if on cue, the front door swung open to reveal Kevin. Becky shook her head and chuckled, "Speak of the devil and his imps will appear."

Kevin cocked his head in a quizzical look.

"Sheila just asked if you were coming by this evening. Hasn't she instructed you to submit your itinerary to her in triplicate at the beginning of the week?" Her aquamarine earrings twinkled nearly as much as her eyes in the soft light.

"Slipped my mind," he said, feigning penitence not very convincingly. "You're looking your usual lovely self tonight, Becky. You do wonderful things for that dress."

Becky did a twirl, the deep apricot crepe flowing softly after her, ending in a small curtsy. "Thank you, kind sir."

Kevin enjoyed the graciously levelheaded way Becky accepted his compliments. It wasn't as if she needed his approval. She knew how people reacted to her beauty and charm, but she seemed genuinely delighted when he took notice and said so. "Full moon tonight," he said, pointing to the window. "Saves on lamp oil, you know."

"Well, as my grandmother used to say, 'waste not, want not.'"

Kevin chortled. "Mine had a rhyme that went: Use it up, wear it out, make it do or do without. You wouldn't catch her wasting lamp oil on a night with a full moon."

"Well, I wouldn't waste a full moon by standing here exchanging folklore," Sheila commented dryly as she approached the register. "Hi, Kevin. Becky, I'll watch the register. You go change."

"That's the best offer I've had this evening," Becky sighed. "My feet have had all of these glass slippers they can enjoy." She squeezed Kevin's arm. "Be back shortly."

"Quite a gal, isn't she?" Sheila observed as Becky disappeared up the stairs.

"I can't say I've ever known anyone quite like her," Kevin said. "Have you known her a long time? You seem very close."

"We've been friends since second grade," Sheila explained, "and that's a good many years now. You can't go through the traumas of growing up together without getting close. Even while she was away, we talked regularly by phone. I don't know what I would have done without her during my postdivorce period."

"Sheila, it's hard for me to believe anyone is as well-balanced as Becky seems to be," Kevin said with a note of rueful skepticism. "I know you're her friend, but is she for real?"

"What you see is pretty much what you get with Becky, Kevin. Of course, she has warts like the rest of us mortals, but you probably won't see them until you know her better, and by then you won't care." Sheila appraised him frankly. "She says you're good for her, and I believe it. She's a happy woman these days, Kevin, in great part due to your influence. Whatever you're doing for her, keep it up." The brown eyes trained on him were a match for the strength of his own gaze. "Kevin, give me a straight answer on this—do you think we're due for another fish kill? Becky doesn't like to talk about it, but I know she's worried."

"To be honest about it, Sheila, I tend to think so, but it's more of a gut conviction than a scientific conclusion. One kill doesn't make a pattern, so I don't have anything solid to go on. I have my fingers crossed against it, but that's not very scientific, either." He jammed his fists into his pants pockets. "I hate this waiting for the other shoe to drop, but I don't know what else we can do at this point," he sighed in frustration.

Sheila combed her fingers through the short blond hair as she rubbed the back of her neck wearily. After a silent moment, she smiled up at Kevin. "I'm just glad you're here, Kevin." She glanced at her watch. "Oops, magic time," she said, roping off the now-empty dining room. "Time to put my feet up and listen to music until I'm needed or closing time, whichever comes first." She locked the register and dropped the key into a wall sconce nearby. "Enjoy the moon," she tossed over her shoulder as she walked toward the door to the club room.

"You've been visiting with Sheila," Becky observed as she bounced down the stairs in jeans and tank top. "Isn't she something? Not many people are lucky enough to have a friend like Sheila. I can't imagine what I've done to deserve it, but I certainly know enough to appreciate what I have."

"I gather the feeling is mutual," Kevin said, opening the door. As they walked down the path in silence, fingers comfortably entwined, Kevin thought about the vigil they were keeping. He had told Sheila the truth, he still thought another kill was probable. But, to tell himself the truth, Kevin knew he wanted to be here with this woman for no more than the pleasure of her company. Over the years he'd learned to mistrust first impressions, but getting to know Becky better had reinforced his first impressions. Apparently she was what she seemed to be, even though she sometimes seemed too good to be true.

When Kevin leaned into the car for the quilt, he emerged first with something he'd propped carefully in the corner of the back seat. When he turned, he handed Becky an antique milk bottle full of wild honeysuckle, the sweet fragrance wafting toward her on the summer night. "They smell so sweet," he explained, "and I hadn't seen any close by here, so...."

"Summer's sweetest flower," she said, quietly inhaling the aroma issuing from the creamy yellow and white trumpets. "Thanks, Kevin. Let's take them with us."

They spread the quilt and sat quietly, Becky tucked between his legs, her knees and the honeysuckle under her chin, his arms wrapped around her. Kevin rested his chin on her shoulder and gently tugged at her earring with his lips. "A penny for your thoughts," he murmured close to her ear.

"Too fat, happy, and lazy to be thinking," she purred.

"May I ask you a question and get an honest answer?" he said softly.

"If I can claim the same privilege," she said, laying her head against his shoulder.

"Have you ever thought about making love with me, Becky? You don't have to answer if you don't want to, of course."

She straightened her head and looked into the distance. For an instant she was very still, and Kevin worried about having brought up the topic too soon. Slowly she raised one hand to rest the long fingers against the side of his face, still looking away from him. "Of course I've thought about it, Kevin. I've even dreamed about it. That doesn't necessarily mean I'm ready to let my mind involve the rest of my body yet." She shifted her position to face him. "Kevin, if things keep moving in the present direction, I have little doubt I'll want to make that commitment one day, but that's how I view it...as a commitment...and I'm not ready just yet."

Kevin sighed melodramatically. "Well, I figure it never hurts to ask."

"Nope, but one of these first days, you won't need to ask," she said, burying her smile in the fragrant flowers for a moment. "Is it time for my question now?"

"Fire away," he said, "but hold my hand. I may need fortification."

Becky set the flowers aside gently and took his extended hand, trying to frame her question carefully. Taking a deep breath, she looked at him squarely. "Kevin, do you trust me enough to tell me the rest of the truth about why you turned your life around so drastically?"

The sudden hard look in his eyes made her fear she had crossed some invisible trip wire that would close all the gates he had opened to her. She persisted, "It's so important to you, I'd like to understand it better."

For a long moment Kevin searched Becky's open face, wondering what prompted her to ask such a question. He remembered Sheila's saying "What you see is pretty much what you get" and accepted her explanation. Still, did he trust her enough to expose the raw place he kept so carefully covered with his bandage of logic and amiability? He wanted to tell her, but could he? He had kept it locked tightly away for so long. He shifted his gaze from her face and crossed his legs to sit tailor fashion. "You ask tougher questions than I do, lady."

"You don't have to answer either," she reminded him softly.

"I know," he replied, looking into the distance, "but I think I want to try, Becky." He took a deep breath, held it for a moment and exhaled it with audible force. "Most of my time with the oil industry was spent in exploration and development. I was in on the early stages of drilling, installation of facilities, refineries, and so forth. I worked mostly in the Middle East, helping underdeveloped countries tap what was sometimes the only source of wealth they owned. It was exciting to me to watch high-rise buildings, water systems, hospitals going up in the desert, knowing petro dollars were paying for the improvements. I really felt good about our contribution to progress, to what I felt sure would be a higher standard of living for the native peoples." He looked down at his boots, a crooked smile twisting his lips. "I got so good at my jobs, so thoroughly versed in the industry, I was transferred to South America to troubleshoot existing installations."

He glanced at Becky sidelong. "Have you ever been to South America?" When she shook her head, he continued. "Neither had I, so I read everything I could get my hands on about the area—the geography, the petroleum economy, the people and how they lived. I got on the plane expecting to land among quaint native people whose houses stood on stilts like storks in a lake where they lived by fishing in the cool, clear mountain waters. I expected to see a veritable paradise of facilities for them, courtesy of thirty years of petroleum development and income."

Abruptly, he got to his feet, shoving his fists into his pockets, and looked down at Becky, a rigid, angry figure. "When the plane started the landing approach at the basin, I looked down to see a huge lake glittering in the sun, covered with rows of what looked to be thousands of sailboats. It was a thrilling picture from the air." He smiled bitterly. "When I got closer, the sailboats turned out to be oil derricks, six thousand plus of them, and the water glittered because of the petroleum staining its surface. Instead of stilted huts on the lake, the natives lived in squalid shanties perched around the lake like deserted stork nests." His head drooped as he flexed his shoulders against the vision. "As for the fish I thought they would be catching to eat"—he snorted scornfully—"they came imported in tins distributed by the government because nothing could live in that lake."

He knelt to face Becky, his face twisted by his memories. "Becky, that whole enormous lake, over six thousand square miles of fresh water, was as dead as it could ever be. The fish were dead, the birds gone, the people transformed by government handouts into useless parasites. It suddenly struck me like a falling meteor, Becky, this was how it all ended, all the high hopes I built into starting all those projects. When the oil ran out, as it certainly will, the situation would be infinitely worse, the people I wanted to help more doomed than ever.

"Becky, I waded into that lake, and I couldn't see my own feet by the time the water reached my knees," he moaned, tears forming in his eyes, "and as I walked away, I met an Indian woman carrying a pail of drinking water from the community tap. Her people had lived for generations at the edge of a freshwater lake too large to see to the opposite shores, and she had to carry drinking water from a common hydrant graciously provided by the government water system only a half mile from her hovel. I watched her mix it with a protein supplement that would keep her family lean but alive. She didn't look much like the full-cheeked pictures in the encyclopedia. I stood there for a moment, too stunned even to cry. Then I walked straight into my office, booked the next flight out, and left my resignation with the secretary."

Becky reached out for Kevin's hands, tears coursing down her own cheeks at his pain. She couldn't speak, only repeatedly swallow against the hard lump in her throat.

"Becky, I spent fifteen years as part of a conspiracy to murder this earth and its creatures," he croaked in agony, "to cripple people with no defense against the technology I inflicted on them, to set their own governments against them by feeding insatiable greed. That

awful realization is my adrenal gland, Becky. It drives
me with a vengeance to do whatever I can do to make
up for those years.''

Becky's fingers brushed away the moisture glistening
on Kevin's cheeks and held her arms wide to him. For
a long time they sat in silence, clinging to each other as
their emotions surged and ebbed, their tears mingling
into a distillation of shared pain and trust that nour-
ished their budding commitment.

"Time for you to leave me to my shift," he said at
last. "Go get some sleep."

"I'd really like to stay," she insisted quietly.

"Not tonight. We'll watch together tomorrow night,
okay? You can take Sunday," he resisted firmly.

Becky agreed reluctantly, mostly because she sensed
his need for solitude following their intense closeness.
Giving him a last kiss, she trudged wearily up the hill
alone.

It was nearly three in the morning when Kevin reached
his apartment, emotionally drained but curiously satisfied. It had been so long since he had someone he
could let into the crevices in his mind and soul. Someone with a touch as light as Becky's, a sensibility as
keen. He felt closer to her at this moment than if they
had simply made physical love without the mating of
their deepest feelings.

As he lay in his bed waiting for sleep, Kevin worried
about the effect on Becky and her parents of another
fish kill. He admitted to ambivalent feelings about it.
He never wanted to see fish die or people like the Shermans hurt, but he couldn't solve the problem for them

until it happened again. He knew how well he could function when the methodical detecting began, but it couldn't begin with what they had to go on now. And, more critical to Kevin, the person responsible couldn't be tracked down and punished for his or her crimes against the fish and the people who depended on the fish to live.

"What are we going to do when winter comes?" Kevin asked idly from his reclining position on the quilt. "I expect it'll be pretty drafty out here at night then."

Becky's laugh tinkled in the pale night. The moon still spilled its largess, scarcely past its prime, over the silent farm. It was a land of monochromactic light and shadow. "My bedroom window has a similar view," she reassured him in a husky voice.

"Why don't I come up and see it some time?" he offered hopefully.

"Did you know your eyes turn silver under a full moon?" she observed, changing the subject abruptly.

"Do you know what it means when an Irishman's eyes turn silver under a full moon?" he asked ominously.

Becky's eyes widened in mock fear. "No. What does it mean?"

"Beats me. I thought you might know." He shrugged cheerfully, dodging her pulled punch.

"I never even knew an Irishman, but all the Irish in my picture books had red hair. What happened to you?" She giggled, running her fingers through his thick ebony locks.

"It's not what happened to me," he explained patiently, "it's that those illustrators thought red looked better with shamrock green. I'll have you know the original settlers of Ireland were Milesians from Spain, and the very best of them looked very much like me. Well, maybe not so refined and handsome, but the coloring was similar at any rate."

"Well, wherever you got it, I like it," Becky growled deep in her throat, "silver eyes and all. Kiss me you latter day leprechaun."

He pulled her down beside him. "I thought you'd never ask." He kissed her gently at first, luring her closer with her own desire, then with his growing urgency. Becky pressed herself along his length, feeling the firm muscles of his compact body against her soft contours. She began to relax, to open herself to the sensations demanding her attention. She could hear their heartbeats mingled with the small noises of the night, the sound of Kevin's hair rustling under her hands, and another sound disturbed her when it reached the interpretive centers of her brain. She sat bolt upright, her ears straining into the surrounding stillness.

"Becky, what's wrong?"

She quickly placed her fingers over his lips. "Shhh. Listen."

He sat up quickly, stared in the direction she indicated and heard it, too. "The fish!"

"The sounds are wrong, Kevin. They're agitated." She jumped to her feet. "Something's wrong."

Simultaneously they realized what was wrong. Becky grabbed Kevin's arm. "I'll call Dad. You go open the gates and let the trout into the big fishout pond. They'll be less crowded. Maybe they'll have a better chance."

They started in opposite directions, scrambling along the steep hillside in the eerie moonlight. "Kevin! After you open the gates, throw the pump switches on the power poles," she shouted at his retreating figure. He threw up an arm in acknowledgment and kept moving.

Becky tore open the back door and dialed her dad's number quickly. "Dad, get down to the ponds. It's happening again, right now." She hung up the phone without waiting for an answer and ran back down the path to the ponds.

The gates were open on the first pond and the night hummed with the splashing drone of the aerator pumps as they spewed water into the air to oxygenate it. Kevin was running from the hatchery building toward the pond with sample jars in his hands. "Becky," he shouted as he saw her coming, "throw boards, sticks, anything like that into this pond. Whatever it is will be absorbed and leave traces."

At a run Becky gathered up a cardboard box, slats from a packing crate, and several small limbs near the bank and threw them into the water. The headlights of Gene's truck as he pulled in picked out several silver bellies in the affected pond.

"The other ponds are okay," Kevin exclaimed loudly. "Get as many as you can into the other ponds."

Becky ran for nets while Gene and Kevin waded into the cold water, not even taking time to don waders. The trout were frantic, churning the surface with their efforts to find oxygen being consumed by the unknown terror in the water. With seine nets, the three determined people forced the frenzied fish toward the gates and into the large fishout pond. They worked like implacable machines, their limbs numbing from the cold, their minds numbing as they struggled to pry loose the cold fingers of death gripping the life in the pond.

When dawn arrived, the grim trio climbed from the water to survey the outcome of the night's labors. Less than a hundred white bellies floated near the gates on the first pond, now deadly still except for the aerator sucking oxygen for inhabitants long gone. In the fish-out pond, the fish had settled down, swimming and breathing normally.

In the silence of total exhaustion, they piled into Gene's truck and drove to his house. Frances met them at the door, wrapping blankets around their shivering and dripping forms. "I built a fire in the fireplace," she said as she passed out mugs of steaming soup and coffee with brandy in it. "Go sit by it while you eat."

Obediently they trudged into the living room to warm their numb feet by the fire. "Don't recall ever having a fire in June," Gene remarked with a small smile, "but it sure feels good, doesn't it?"

"We saved most of them, Mother," Becky said flatly as she sipped at the sturdy soup, "but it was quite a night."

"This time, though, we'll get the bastards," Kevin said with suppressed fury. "We were there when it happened, and we'll find out what caused it."

Frances flashed shock at Kevin's raw expression, turning quickly to bring more coffee. He seemed like such a nice young man, too, was her thought as her lips set tightly.

Gene's face was drawn and haggard. He got stiffly to

his feet. "If it hadn't been for you two, we could have lost them all. Thanks, Kevin, Becky. I think I'll get some rest now." Frances helped him to the bedroom. "I'm too old for this sort of thing," he was saying as he closed the door behind them.

"Come on, honey," Kevin said, pulling Becky up and holding her for a moment, his mask of geniality securely back in place. "You'd better get some rest, too." As they walked toward the restaurant, he held the blanket around her soaked body. "We'll get them this time, Becky, I promise. Call me when you get up, and we'll map out our campaign. I'll pick up the samples on the way out and get to work on them."

They walked in through the kitchen and to Becky's stairway. "Shall I see you to bed?" Kevin asked.

"Please," Becky nodded.

They climbed the stairs, leaning on each other. When they reached the bedroom door, Becky opened it and turned to Kevin, a smile lighting up her otherwise bedraggled countenance. "Thanks for being here, Kevin . . . for the fish, for Dad, and most of all for me."

He smoothed her tangled tresses and kissed her gently. "Any time, Becky. Get some rest and I'll talk to you later today." He turned to go.

"Kevin"—she turned him again with his name—"I really do treasure you, you know."

He nodded, a grin wreathing his weary face, blew her another kiss and disappeared down the stairs into the morning.

The sun rode high in the sky when Becky finally awoke. She lay still, tentatively stretching first one arm, then the other, gingerly cracking her vertebrae into alignment and wondering if she could get as far as the shower. Only by shuffling, she quickly discovered as she made her way to the bathroom. When she emerged from the hot shower some fifteen minutes later, she could manage a slow stroll with not too many signs of visible distress. She wondered how her father would be feeling this morning. The night had nearly disabled her, and Gene was twenty-five years older than she.

She dressed in cool cotton drawstring pants and a loose smock top. While she brushed her hair, she decided to call Kevin, to see how he was faring. The phone rang just as she laid her hand on it. "Hello?"

"When are you going to haul your pretty fanny out of that bed?" Kevin's deep voice greeted her.

"This must be an obscene phone call. What's it to you if I didn't exactly bounce out of bed with a song today?" she retorted gruffly.

His deep chuckle tickled her ear. "I was a little stiff myself this morning, but us old guys are tough. Anyway, I'm having coffee with the other old guy because I got tired of waiting for you to call. Your mother says she's keeping breakfast warm for you."

"Be down in a minute." Becky smiled to herself and hung up. Her first thought was to walk, but negotiating the stairs cured her of that frivolous notion. She took the car to her parents' back door.

When Becky entered, Frances started filling her plate. Gene and Kevin had long since finished all but their coffee. Becky gave Gene a quick kiss and a hard look. "How are you this morning, Dad?"

A slow grin crumpled his face. "I feel like I've been

rode hard and put away wet, that's how. Can't do that sort of thing like I could thirty years ago. How about you?''

"I decided to get up when I realized I'd have to get better to die," Becky groaned, sitting stiffly, "and I wasn't showing any signs of improvement."

"Boy, this younger generation sure is soft," Kevin teased, his blue eyes crackling.

"Many more nights like last night, and I'll be in the older generation," Becky countered. "Thanks, Mother," she said, taking the plate heaped with scrambled eggs, sausage, and biscuits. "Listen, old soldier"—she pointed a fork at Kevin—"while I get my strength up here, you start mapping out our strategy or tactics or whatever you toughies call it. What do we do first?''

"First thing we do is run all the tests and try to identify the substance. I stopped by the lab on the way here, and the water samples are underway. I'm also going to try to extract any traces from the boards we threw in last night. If it's a petrochemical, the wood will absorb some of it."

Becky buttered a biscuit. "Then what?"

"Then we start the hard part, trying to get the authorities off their collective duffs to help us track down the polluter," Kevin said with a notable lack of enthusiasm.

"Yeah, run up the phone bill and my blood pressure all for an encore on the song and dance we got the first time," Becky jeered, taking a bite of the biscuit. She chewed thoughtfully. "Dad, you have any ideas?"

"Nope," Gene sighed. "If we find out what's going on and we can't get the authorities to deal with it, I don't know where we go from there. I guess I could talk to some of the city councilmen. I know most of them, but I don't know what they could do unless they had proof somebody was dumping illegally.'' He set his cup down. ''I don't have any experience with this, Beck. I don't know what to do.''

Gene knew all there was to know about trout—how to spawn them, how to grow them, how to take care of them, how to cook them. But Becky realized he was on alien territory here. ''Kevin?''

''Look, I'm a scientist by profession and by temperament. I can take care of the testing, detecting, tracking down the substance, but once I have the information, somebody else will have to take over. I am not a politician, nor do I choose to be.'' He leaned his elbows on the table. ''If this is illegal dumping, and I'm sure it is, somebody is making money out of it. They'll do everything possible to prevent our upsetting their arrangement. That's where politics usually comes into it, and that's where I bow out. I spent too many years being and seeing the victims of political maneuvering. The older I get, the lower my tolerance for all the bullroar,'' he finished sourly.

''There's also the little matter of who signs your paycheck,'' Becky added, ''and the city might not appreciate an employee snooping around in their records for unauthorized reasons.''

''I was looking for a job when I found this one''—Kevin shrugged indifferently—''but a low profile would make me more useful. Just tell me what you want to know and I'll get it.''

Frances stood quietly dispensing coffee until this

point in the conversation. "Becky, I'm not sure you ought to put Kevin up to spying or anything, and I'm not sure you ought to start anything that might end up being dangerous. If what Kevin says is true, it could happen, couldn't it?"

Before Becky could respond, Gene took his wife's hand. "Frances, I think we can trust these two to proceed carefully and do whatever is best for the farm. We'll do whatever we can to help, but I'm willing to leave it to them. Becky is a grown woman who will own this farm one day. She might as well start practicing right now."

"Still sounds too dangerous for a woman." Frances fidgeted.

Inwardly Becky groaned at her mother's stubborn refusal to accept Becky's decisions about her life. Frances still couldn't comprehend why Becky would rather run a restaurant than raise a houseful of kids and often reminded her time was running out for her.

"Mother, this is our hometown, not some Mafia stronghold. This is a new time, and there are laws about pollution. Detective work in this case isn't like on television. No guns, just slowly tracking down and documenting infractions. We'll start by assuming the proper authorities will act on it if we get the evidence they need. Nobody wants people going around dumping poisons indiscriminately. I sincerely believe we can put a stop to it if we do our homework."

"Well, I feel better about Kevin's helping you with it," Frances sniffed, unconvinced.

"For different reasons, so do I," Becky agreed. "Let's keep this quiet as long as we can. I don't think fish kills would be too good for business." She swallowed the last of her coffee. "Let's walk off some soreness and do our plotting, Kevin."

"Thanks for breakfast, Mrs. Sherman," Kevin said with a smile. "Don't worry, we'll take care of each other."

They walked slowly down the hill to the ponds. The crystal clear water was peaceful, its inhabitants swimming on their usual rounds. Except for the still unburied fish on the bank, there was little evidence of the life and death struggle enacted through the previous night. Kevin put his arm around Becky as they walked. "Call Pollution Control tomorrow and report the kill to them. Tell them what we did and that samples are being tested in the university lab. There's not much else you can do until I know what the substance is. I'll run the lab work as soon as I can get to it."

She wrapped her arm around his waist, tucking her hand in his pants pocket. "I don't know what we would have done without you last night, Kevin. Thanks for being here." She looked at the ground as they walked. "Will you answer one question for me honestly?"

"I'll certainly try," he replied, remembering what happened the last time she said that and bracing himself.

"Would you have stayed with me last night if you hadn't thought this was going to happen?" Her voice was solemn and carefully neutral.

Kevin stopped walking and pulled her around to face him. "I thought we'd already settled that," he chided her gently. "I was here to be with you, and we sat outside on the hill because we both wanted to be near the fish. I plan to be around long enough to clear up any lingering doubts, but I'll just have to ask you to trust me until then."

She grinned up at him in tired belief. "I don't see why you wouldn't be good at politics with answers like that." She planted a kiss on his lips. "I'm still tired, I know you have to be, and tomorrow is a work day. Neither of us will rest if we're with each other, so go home and I'll see you tomorrow, sweet man."

"Do you think we can make it back up the hill to our cars?" he groaned, looking up wanly.

"Honey, we can do anything as long as we got each other to lean on," Becky said with vigor. "And a lot of places to rest along the way," she added with a weak smile as they set off toward the house.

Chapter Six

"Might as well have been a recording," Becky fumed as she slammed down the receiver after hearing the same person at Pollution Control say precisely the same thing he said when she called two weeks before. They couldn't accept her samples, but they would send someone out. "What a way to start a week."

The week didn't improve much with age until Kevin called late on Wednesday, excitement in his voice. "Becky, I think I've got it. I have a couple more tests to run, but I think I know what it is now."

"Well, tell me," she prompted him impatiently.

"Not until I'm absolutely sure, but I wanted you to know these aren't coming up negative. I'll call you again the minute they're done. By the way, I've missed you the last couple of days. You have a high addictive index, you know," he teased.

"Thank you, I think," she laughed. "Things have been pretty dull around here, too, except for a stimulating replay of my prior conversation with Pollution Control."

"Hang in there," Kevin admonished her before hanging up.

Becky almost wished he had waited to call until he had something to tell her. He sounded so excited that it must be something significant. She worried about it while she worked.

Just before closing time, Kevin dashed into the deserted dining room waving a sheaf of computer printouts. His eyes crackled with enthusiasm. "I've got it," he repeated, dragging Becky to the table in the corner and spreading out the papers. "There was nothing in the fish, no traces of anything in the fatty tissues, so we're not dealing with heavy metals or toxins. That's good news. The water tests didn't show up a lot, although I did find traces of solvents and oil."

"Kevin," Becky shrieked in frustration, "don't tell me what you didn't find, tell me what you did."

"Sorry," he said with a twinkle, "I get carried away sometimes. What I did find were heavy traces of petroleum in the wood we threw into the pond that night. That tells us we're probably dealing with petroleum-based waste, very likely contaminated lubricating oils, waste oils and the like, with miscellaneous wastes mixed in."

Becky stared at Kevin. "But doesn't every factory produce that kind of stuff, Kevin? How are we ever going to trace something like that back to a specific source?"

"Glad you asked." He grinned. "I'm going to run a chromatography test that will give us the fingerprint of the oil, my dear."

"Oil has fingerprints?" Becky cocked a skeptical eyebrow.

"You'd better believe it does. Texas oil is different from Oklahoma oil and so on. Each has what we call a fingerprint because it's unique to that oil. Once we get the fingerprint, we find out what industries in the area are using what oils, which should narrow the field considerably. The chromatograph will give us a map to compare with all the known standards and any new samples we find. The same wastes will produce identical chromatograms, so as we get new samples, we simply compare them to this one we took from the pond." He grinned triumphantly.

"Sounds like a long, involved process to me," Becky said, shaking her head over the esoteric readouts. "Want a beer? I think I need one."

"Sure, but just a quick one. I have to get back to the lab." He walked to the kitchen with her. "It is a long, involved process, Becky, but that's how we'll get what we want. Tomorrow, go to the mayor and tell him what happened. Ask for records of what substances which industries put into the municipal sewer system." He accepted the cold bottle Becky offered and took a short swig. "Maybe the word will get around that we're on the trail, and maybe whoever is doing it will get spooked enough to quit dumping until we get it all sorted out."

"I'll see the mayor tomorrow. I've known him all my life," she remarked, quickly adding, "Never liked him, but always known him. You keep working on the fingerprints."

"We also have to figure out how it's getting into

your pond. Saturday we need to start walking the area and looking for the most likely dumping area to get the stuff to your place, okay?''

"You got it. I'll get Sheila to cover for me, and we'll take a hike."

"One last thing. I have a good friend who is the mayor's administrative assistant. I'll run this by him and see if he has any ideas for streamlining the bureaucratic bull we have to endure to get what we need." He gulped the remainder of his beer and gathered up his papers.

"Thanks, Kevin," Becky said, squeezing his arm and trying to hide her disappointment as they walked to the door. She wasn't sure what she'd expected, but somehow she thought Kevin might have a more definitive answer. "I really needed the encouragement." She smiled, not wanting to dampen his enthusiasm.

"Don't uncross your fingers just yet," he cautioned with a smile, kissed her quickly, and ran to his car.

Mayor Milam Trimble was about the same age as Gene Sherman, and Becky had known him since childhood, although she hadn't seen him since moving back to Oakdale. He looked up without recognition as she entered his office but smiled broadly at the sound of her name. "How are you, Rebecca? Sit down and tell me how Gene and Frances are getting along."

Becky inquired after the mayor's family, too, and the first few minutes of the interview were given over to exchanging personal information, but Mayor Trimble soon asked what brought Becky to see him.

"Let me see if I can summarize a fairly long story for

you, Mr. Trimble," she said, briefly explaining what had happened at the farm, what steps they had taken to locate the source, and what they had learned. "So, Mr. Trimble, I need to know what substances are going into the sewer system from what industries and how much each industry is allowed. We may be able to get a lead from that."

The mayor cleared his throat loudly. "Rebecca, I can't tell you how sorry I am about what happened. Gene's a good man, and I know how he feels about his fish. I have to tell you, though, I think you're barking up the wrong tree. All the industry in Oakdale is nice clean industry, and they're all real careful about meeting all the standards."

"Isn't it possible that one might have more waste than they're allowed to put through the city system?"

"Well"—the mayor rubbed his earlobe uneasily—"anything is possible, I suppose, but I'm sure they would make adequate arrangements for disposal. Rebecca, be careful what you imply about our manufacturing plants. They're a little touchy right now. The state and federal governments have made the city tighten up our standards for municipal waste, and the adjustment has been rough for some of our plants and costly. This new governor has handed us all the problems we can handle right now without worrying about Gene's dead fish. His farm isn't even inside the city limits, and most of our beleaguered plants are."

Becky remembered why she never liked Trimble. "If they're under such unbearable pressures, Mr. Mayor, it would seem even more likely someone may be cutting costs by dumping their excess in a manner not up to standards, wouldn't it? If they aren't, surely they won't mind someone asking the question, will they?"

Trimble's eyebrows knit into a scowl. "Now, Rebecca, don't got stirring up trouble where there isn't any. We've worked long and hard to bring industry here so our people would have jobs. With unemployment as high as it is nationwide, there would be communities lined up around the block for a chance at our plants."

Becky watched his lecture incredulously, wondering whose side he was on until what he was saying finally dawned on her. "Ah, it's the old jobs-at-any-price dilemma, isn't it?"

He flushed. "That's not what I said, Rebecca. What I am saying is that I won't go prying around in their business for no good reason, and I'd suggest you adopt the same policy. You can't expect the city to help you unless you have something more substantial than suspicions." He stood, indicating the interview was at an end. "Give my regards to your parents, Rebecca."

As she walked away, Becky heard the mayor muttering his amazement of a daughter of Frances Sherman behaving like some hippie environmentalist. Struggling against a desire to wheel around and expound her theory of his lineage, Becky forced herself to continue to Engineering. As she stormed around Kevin's partition, she nearly fell over a tall, bespectacled young man sitting across the desk from Kevin, his feet propped up opposite Kevin's. In contrast to Kevin's casual khakis, the young man wore a neat business suit and one of the worst-looking ties Becky ever saw. "Oh, I'm sorry, Kevin. I didn't know you were busy."

"You're right on cue." Kevin smiled, stepping into the next office to borrow an additional chair. "We were just talking about you. Were your ears burning?"

"Yes, but for a different reason," Becky growled, plopping down into the chair. "The man is a total nitwit who refuses to be of any help whatsoever."

Both men laughed. "Kevin told me you were seeing His Honor this morning," the lanky young man said. "I'm Gordon Yates."

Becky's still-angry eyes regarded him without comprehension until Kevin said, "Trimble's administrative assistant I was telling you about?"

"Oh, I remember. Hi, Gordon. Your boss is a jerk. I thought so when I was a kid, and I still think so," she said flatly. "He assures me none of Oakdale's upright industries would even consider dumping illegally and suggests I not go around making wild accusations that could cause our local unemployment statistics to soar. To summarize, our interview was something less than satisfactory for either of us," she finished, her voice heavy with sarcasm.

"I hope you didn't vote for him," Kevin grinned. "Now you know why cities hire administrative assistants to handle business instead of relying on elected officials."

"Trimble suffers from a bad case of what I privately call the Chamber of Commerce mentality," Gordon commented laconically. "By that I mean he is a partisan of growth at any price, because to him growth means jobs and jobs ensure his prestige. It never seems to register with the progrowth people that one of the reasons industry is leaving the Northeast is because pollution standards have become to tough for them there. This threat of a moratorium has thrown everyone into a panic, Becky. Frankly I doubt if the mayor cares where anything is dumped, so long as it isn't into the municipal sewer.''

"They used to come just for cheap labor," Becky observed wryly, "but now they get the extra bonus of lower standards and higher profits. What more could they ask?"

"Well, for the most part we've been lucky here," Gordon said. "We've gone after clean industry to begin with, and we've had good cooperation from the majority on our new standards for effluent. From what Kevin says, it looks like there may be a rotten apple in the barrel that needs to be tossed, though." He swung his long legs off the desk. "If anything I say in this office today comes back on me, I'll deny even knowing either one of you. Clear?"

"Fair enough," they agreed.

His casual demeanor changed to brisk efficiency. "Kevin, I'd suggest you stay out of this, except for doing your testing. Since you are not the injured party, and since you draw a paycheck from the city, a low profile is your best course. You're not likely to win any popularity contests around here anyway, especially now that the state has threatened the city with what you've championed all along. Becky, I have to come up with a sewer plan inside the next thirty days, so I don't have time to go through a lot of records on a spook chase, but I can give you one piece of information that will get you access to what you need. This state has a Freedom of Information Act that says, in effect, that any entity using public monies must open its records to any tax-payer requesting to see them, providing they don't deal with personnel or national security." He paused to let the implications sink in. "If the taxpayer finds any re-luctance to produce such records, all the taxpayer needs to do is state her intention to go to court under the Freedom of Information Act for an opinion." He grinned unexpectedly. "Generally that will loosen ev-erything right up." Smoothing his atrocious tie, Gor-don stood to leave. "Nice to meet you, Becky, and I assume I will be seeing you again soon."

"Thanks, Gordon." Kevin grinned as the lean form disappeared through the door.

"He's wonderful," Becky chortled. "I wonder why such a bright, capable person would wear a tie like that."

Kevin laughed heartily. "That's exactly what I asked him as soon as I knew him well enough. He wears them all the time. I don't even know where he finds that many awful ties, but he manages. He's the frontline flak-catcher for city hall, you know, and he says he wears the ties as a diversionary tactic. Either they dis-tract whoever is trying to chew him up, or the person feels uncomfortable about being ugly to anybody sim-ple enough to wear something like that."

"Simple like a dodecahedron," Becky snorted.

"Rebecca! Where did you learn a word like that?" Kevin asked.

"Solid geometry," she retorted, "which I took be-fore I found out girls weren't supposed to be good at math."

"Listen, I'm spending all afternoon in the lab. I

found a guy in Chemistry to help me run the fingerprint tests, and I hope we'll have something by tomorrow. What's on your itinerary?''

"I'm going to visit a few of the city council members
who know Dad well and see if we can't generate a little
support to draw on when the time comes. As soon as
you have the test results, I'll go to Gordon and request
the records on what's going into the sewer system.''
Her shoulders sagged. "To be honest, Kevin, I hadn't
realized until today that our trout would be up against
people's jobs. That sort of puts us on an uphill course,
doesn't it?''

"I'm afraid so,'' he nodded, "but it's a hill we have
to climb, isn't it? I'm a little surprised your Washington experience didn't prepare you better for these
kinds of games, Becky.''

She stood to go. "I'm beginning to think my education wasn't as broad as it seemed when I was getting
it,'' she sighed. "Got time to walk me to the door?''

"Thought you'd never ask,'' he teased, jumping
from his chair to take her arm as she walked. "Okay if
we go to dinner tonight?''

"Thought you'd never ask,'' she said with a twinkle.
"See you then.''

"Just a sec,'' he said, sticking his head into an empty
cubbyhole to look around before pulling her in after
him. "One quick kiss to get me through the afternoon.''

"Small fee for a scientist.'' Becky smiled as his lips
descended for a gentle, longing kiss. "I'd better see
you later,'' she whispered, touching his lips with one
long finger before slipping out of his arms.

It was nearly opening time at Rainbow's End when Becky got home from her afternoon of running down councilmen. They all seemed sympathetic, probably because of their friendship with Gene, but they found it hard to believe that any of the local industries would deliberately dump pollutants illegally. To a man, they assured her they would do what they could if she came up with any definite proof against an industry. They cautioned her that it would need to be definite to get much attention from a council worrying over the state's threat of a moratorium if they didn't have a satisfactory sewer plan within thirty days.

After showering, Becky lay on the bed to rest a few minutes before dressing. She chided herself for her history of political smugness. Until now, Becky had never considered environmental problems a high priority, concentrating instead only on her own narrow professional concerns. Ruefully she wondered how many other people were like her, content to bury their heads in the sand until somebody slapped the part of their anatomy left exposed by such a posture. Becky vowed the pain in her posterior would never again allow her to drift into the comfortable apathy that made such tragic travesties possible.

Kevin arrived just after eight, glowing with excitement. He grabbed Becky's hand as he headed for their table. "We got it, sweetheart. This time we got it."

"Got what?" Becky asked as she skipped to keep up with his forward charge.

He slapped the sheaf of papers down on the table, which fortunately was never set until needed. "We've traced it down to a specific petroleum product that is not all that common. Not more than half a dozen industries in this area would be using it, and it's probably fewer than that. The city has fairly detailed information about which industries discharge what into the city system, and this particular waste is one that would be subject to city standards for amounts discharged.''

Becky hugged him enthusiastically. "I'll be in Gordon's office first thing in the morning to go through those records. Oh, Kevin, we finally have something specific to go on."

"Don't get too excited yet. We still have a long hike ahead of us."

"True, but we have less than we did yesterday," she reminded him cheerfully. "How's your appetite? You've just restored mine."

"This is the stuff that dreams are made of," Kevin smiled. "Not only is this lady beautiful, charming, intrepid, et cetera... she owns a restaurant specializing in handouts to struggling college students. However, my dear, we are going out to celebrate tonight."

"Kevin, we don't have to go out to celebrate," she protested. "Besides, I'm working tonight."

"I know we don't have to, but we're going anyway," he insisted. "As for your working, Gene and Sheila can cover for you. Right, Gene?"

Becky turned to see her father coming through the door. He couldn't stay out of the kitchen, dropping in occasionally to see to the broiling of the trout, even after Becky hired a regular cook. It was his favorite dish, one he developed, prepared on equipment specially constructed to his design. "Right. You two look like cats with a key to the canary shop. What's going on?''

"Must be good news if she's eating out again," Sheila quipped as she swung through the kitchen door with an order, which she handed to the cook with the added instruction to watch Gene's trout so he could stay in the dining room with Becky and Kevin.

"Dad, just wait until you hear what Kevin has for us," Becky fairly bubbled. "Kevin, wait until Sheila gets back. I want her to hear, too."

"It must be good," Gene chuckled. "Her visit with Mayor Trimble sure didn't produce this reaction." He shook his head ruefully. "I told her not to put any eggs in that basket."

"Shiela," Becky called as her friend reappeared, "come listen to this."

Kevin briefly reiterated his findings for the assembly, despite Becky's enthusiastic interpolations. "So, we haven't solved the problem by any means," he concluded, "but we finally have something sufficiently specific to be of some use. At least we can start hunting now."

"Well done," Sheila pronounced, kissing Kevin on top of his head. She spotted a customer at the door. "Gotta run. Let me know if I can help any way."

"You figure the problem is confined to the first pond, Kevin?" Gene asked thoughtfully.

"Seems to be, doesn't it?" he replied.

"How do you figure that?"

"That's one of the next things we try to find out, Gene," Kevin said. "Just how it gets into that pond."

"I think it has to be coming from the creek behind the hill," Becky offered. "Dad, you know how that creek goes underground in places? I think it takes the stuff with it.''

Gene studied for a moment. ''Well, there are cracks and faults all through this flintrock ground. I don't suppose it would be too unlikely that one connected that creek with our pond, would it?''

''I'd say it's pretty likely,'' Kevin agreed. ''Becky, I won't have any time until Saturday, but let's do some prowling around that creekbed to see what we can find.''

''Nice weather for a hike in the woods.'' She smiled.

''Well, I'd better get back to my grill,'' Gene said, standing. ''Keep me posted. Take it easy, Kevin, and thanks.''

''Take it easy, he says,'' Becky giggled. ''You're wound up like an eight-day clock, and my imperturbable father says take it easy.''

''You're not exactly sedate yourself,'' Kevin retorted. ''Let's be on our way. Dinner, wine, candlelight, then I have a superb idea for relaxing if you can get your mind off business for a while.''

''I'll just bet you do,'' Becky said with a grin as he ushered her to the door.

They drove to a quiet little restaurant in a nearby community settled by Italian immigrants and known for superb food and wine. The plump, darkly pretty waitress showed them to a corner table at Kevin's request. The atmosphere was quiet, softly lit, and apparently lost on Becky. ''Kevin,'' she said thoughtfully, ''I'm going to call the state tomorrow and tell them what we have. Maybe they can start getting us some answers.''

Kevin shook his head, sighing loudly. ''Candlelight,

soft music, a devastatingly charming companion, and all the lady can talk about is business. I must be losing it in my waning years."

Becky hung her head in momentary apology. "Sorry, but it's worrying me to death. I'll hush in a minute. What do you think about calling them?"

"Don't do it," he responded briefly. "We don't have enough yet. Call them if and when we find the source."

"But that could take so long," she said urgently, leaning across the table, the candlelight gilding her dark features. "I'm not willing to wait, Kevin. They are the ones who should be out searching for the source, checking factory records, that's their job, not ours."

Kevin nodded wearily. "They should be doing a lot of things, Becky, but you and I both know they're probably not going to do any of them by your timetable. Why the sudden resentment? Thirty minutes ago you were all ready to spend Saturday prowling that creek from one end to the other to find the source."

"I still am," she said defensively, "but the more I think about it, the angrier I get. Why should we have to pay taxes and still do their dirty work for them? It's just not right, Kevin."

"We're not talking about right, we're talking about reality," he replied calmly as the waitress brought their order. Kevin started eating while Becky toyed with her food.

"You sure have a lot more patience with them than I do," she huffed, finally sampling the linguini.

"I have more patience with almost everything than you do," he smiled wryly. "Part of that is the scientific mind and a lot more of it comes from having been around enough to know how far the distance between should and is. Tell you what does try my patience, though: your inability to forget about the whole thing long enough to enjoy the here and now, the food, the wine, the music...and me." He regarded her solemnly. "I came here to celebrate. Would you care to join me?"

Impulsively she reached for his hand. "Kevin, I'm sorry, really. I seem to have a one-track mind. All this stuff keeps recycling in my head, and I can't seem to shut it off at will. It's not that I don't try...."

"I know, honey, and I try to understand," he said patiently, lifting his glass to peer at her over the ruby contents. "I just want you to remember all this when my mind gets stuck in one track some day soon"—he grinned mischievously—"and I can guarantee you it won't be on fish and politics."

"Threat or promise?" She smiled over the rim of her wineglass at him, feeling very lucky to be a part of Kevin's here and now and trying her best to push the intrusive thoughts out of her awareness for the evening.

Chapter Seven

Becky affected her best mask of righteous indignation when she confronted Gordon in his office the next morning. "Mayor Trimble refused me access to your records on industrial effluent, Mr. Yates. I am asking you to make them available to me, or I shall be forced to go to court for an opinion under the Freedom of Information Act."

Gordon frowned, but Becky saw a tiny twitch at the corner of his mouth as he stroked his choice of terrible ties for the day. "Well, Ms Sherman, I'm sure Mayor Trimble didn't mean to imply that we have anything to hide, and I'm even more sure he wouldn't want you to take court action. I'll call down to the Water and Sewer office and have the records waiting for you when you get there."

"Thank you for your cooperation, Mr. Yates." She turned briskly on her heel, carefully changing the wink to a frown before reaching Gordon's secretary. As she walked to the Water and Sewer office, Becky felt grateful for people like Gordon Yates. After meeting Gordon and Kevin, she felt somewhat less disillusioned about the tax dollars she put into municipal government.

Becky sat down with a legal pad and the mound of records provided by the clerk in the Water and Sewer office. As she began a systematic perusal of the data, she was amazed and a little appalled at the amount and variety of chemicals and toxic materials being run routinely through the municipal sewer system. She found such toxins as cyanide, mercury, other heavy metals, petrochemicals she recognized, myriad chemicals and compounds she'd never heard of. No wonder the state was on Oakdale's case. Where did it all end up? How did the city treat stuff like that? As the extent of her ignorance dawned on her, Becky realized she didn't even know where the municipal treatment plant was, much less what they did there or where the wastes went after treatment. Probably into the water supply, she thought dismally.

After wading through all the records, Becky had listed on her yellow pad the names of five area industries discharging the particular type of petroleum product Kevin had fingerprinted. She thanked the clerk for her help and walked back to her car, beginning to organize an itinerary to visit each of the five plants. It certainly wouldn't hurt to ask about their waste disposal procedures, would it? The most they could do would be refuse to talk to her.

The first plant assured her there had been no accidental spills. The manager went out of his way to show her their waste disposal records, expressing his sympathy for her losses and his resentment toward the few polluting industries that tarred all of them with the same brush. Becky thanked him for his cooperation and crossed the name off the list as she returned to the car, deciding these people took the pollution standards seriously. She was even a little abashed at having stuck all industrial managers in the same black bag.

At United Industries, a secretary showed her into a spacious office, decorated in plush carpet and leather furniture, and asked her to wait a few minutes until the manager was free. She looked at the carefully selected prints on the walls, wondering if the office's occupant ever looked at them.

"Ms Sherman?" a rather nasal voice addressed her as the door opened behind her. Becky turned to see a bulky man, probably in his early sixties, entering the office in a proprietary fashion. "I'm Douglas Price. What can I do for you today?" He walked to his chair, effectively placing the desk between himself and his visitor.

Becky quickly related the story. "So, what I'm doing is checking with all the area industries using this type of oil to see if anyone has had an accidental spill that would explain our problem."

Price's smile didn't reach his cold gray eyes. "Ms Sherman, if you've been to the city, you must be aware of what tight controls we have over our manufacturing wastes. Surely you don't think a local industry would let an accidental spill go unreported, do you?"

His tone of voice contracted Becky's brow into a frown. "Then it would have to be an intentional dumping, wouldn't it?"

Price's nostrils flared as he reached into his desk drawer. "I suppose you're one of these people who would like to see all industry forced out of business by excessive regulation." He popped a tablet into his mouth. "What would people do for jobs then? We provide one hundred jobs for this community, Ms Sherman. How many people do you employ?"

"It seems to me that is hardly the point here, Mr. Price." Becky stared at him incredulously. "I don't want to deprive people of jobs, but we've had one disaster and one near-disaster at our trout farm, and I intend to find out why. Whoever was responsible should pay for our losses, don't you think?"

He stood abruptly. "United Industries doesn't dump its wastes, Ms Sherman, and I resent your implication that we do. If you'll excuse me, I have work to do."

Becky wouldn't be put off so easily. "Mr. Price, I'll be more than happy to be proved in error. Would you mind if I looked through your records?"

"Our records are available to the proper people on a need-to-know basis," he said with a glare, "but we have enough government people snooping in our records as it is. I have neither time nor inclination to review them with anyone who comes in off the street and wants to see what we're doing."

After considering the rock wall she faced, Becky rose to go. As she reached the door, Price's voice turned her around. "And Ms Sherman, if I were you, I'd think seriously about the possible consequences of accusing people of criminal activity. You could end up in a great deal of difficulty."

Douglas Price popped another antacid tablet into his mouth as he watched the young woman leave his office. Damn her and her trout, he thought angrily.

Charley assured him there was nothing along that creek to hurt. Well, it couldn't be helped. The main office in Chicago wasn't interested in hearing about his problems with the city's new standards; they wanted more production and higher profits. And Douglas Price was too close to retirement to let one girl and some damned fish queer things for him.

He picked up the phone and quickly called the waste hauler with whom he had the phantom deal. "This is Price. I may have a little problem developing, and I want to be sure your records are in order.... Well, be sure you show regular pickups from here in case anyone checks on it. I'm paying for high quality paperwork, and I expect to get what I pay for," he snarled and slammed down the receiver.

He ground another chalky mint between his teeth as he dialed the mayor's office. Price knew he could stampede Milam Milquetoast by merely suggesting he might be looking for a place to move the plant.

Just who the hell did this girl think she was dealing with anyway? He'd give her something to think about besides United Industries and give himself time to be sure he was in the clear. He could toss around innuendo, too. Maybe it would be a good idea to drop the rumor here and there that he'd heard her fancy restaurant served contaminated fish, but he was sure it couldn't be true. He knew the best place to start something like that, too, with no fear of its being traced back to him.

Becky didn't cross United Industries off her list, but she decided to make one more visit before going home. The manager at the next plant on her list was reluctant to talk to her and suggested it was probably the work of a waste hauler. He ranted at length about having to pay through the nose for some pirate to haul off their wastes, only to have him dump it in the nearest creek, leaving the plant holding the bag if it caused a problem. He didn't strike Becky as the type who could easily feign such convincing outrage, but she left him on the list. She thanked him and left with sinking hopes. If it were a waste hauler at the bottom of it, the chances of catching him would be slim indeed.

When she arrived at Rainbow's End, Gene greeted her from his usual station. "Hi, honey. How did your expedition for today go?"

She pecked him on the cheek. "Educational, to say the least. Gordon helped me get around old Trimble for the information we needed."

"Good for him," Gene laughed. "Never did like Milam much. Politics is the first thing he's ever stuck with for long. Went broke at everything else, but the city is probably better capitalized than he usually was."

"I wish I could be so generous," Becky sneered. "The man is a cruelty joke on his constituents, Dad. I sure hope he has some strong opposition I can campaign for in the next election." She poured herself some iced tea. "I think maybe we ought to go to the next City Council meeting and raise a little hell, Dad. What do you think?"

"I don't know about that, sugar. I'm not sure that would be the best thing for business. Probably we ought to keep it quiet until we have the goods on somebody."

"I know," Becky sighed heavily, "but I don't think

most people have the first notion of what's going on in this town. If we don't get the goods pretty soon, I may start screaming at somebody to move it along a little faster. I think maybe the City Council could do it if they wanted to."

"Lord, Beck"—Gene shook his head—"you're going to give your mother a heart attack before this is over."

"She'd have a heart attack if she knew what I know about what's in our drinking water, too," she retorted. "Dad, I don't want to embarrass Mother or anybody else, but I don't intend to sit by demurely while somebody puts us out of business."

"You may be biting off more than you can chew, Beck."

"Could be, Dad, but if I start choking, I want to hear some other people sputtering, too."

"Maybe I'd better practice up on the Heimlich maneuver," Gene said with a grin, returning to his work. "I do admire your spirit, honey, but I can't help worrying a little, too.'

"You two had better worry about getting fired," Sheila gibed as she swung through the kitchen door. "I won't have the help hanging around and visiting when work needs doing." She grinned, then looked Becky over. "Becky, have you forgotten you advertised a live semi-pro singer in the club tonight? You don't look much like what people will be expecting."

"It hadn't crossed my mind," Becky admitted, finishing her tea. "I'll go change right away, Sheila. One more thing, Dad. Do you happen to know a man named Douglas Price? He's about your age and plant manager at United Industries."

Gene thought a minute. "The name doesn't ring a bell, Beck. Why?"

"I talked to him today," Becky explained, "and found him to be a most unpleasant man. His tone was not only defensive, it was downright threatening. I think he bears closer scrutiny."

As Becky left to change, Gene's kindly eyes turned icy as he muttered, "I don't much appreciate people who threaten my family, Sheila. Maybe I need to look into Mr. Price's business a little myself." He continued dressing fish with his experienced knife.

Kevin lounged crookedly in his chair listening to the Waste Management Committee argue over what was to be done about Janice Miller's ultimatum. Several plant managers were there to assure the committee they couldn't possibly afford the proposed higher sewer rates. A gray-haired woman on the committee spoke at last. "Well, someone has to pay for it, and I can't see any way the citizens of this community will stand still for fifty to seventy-five dollar sewer bills. That would bankrupt a lot of our senior citizens, you know."

A plant manager snorted. "Our sewer bill is closer to ten thousand dollars a month."

A young man on the commission responded quickly, "Yes, but you can add that on to the price of the end product. We're talking about people on fixed incomes, Social Security."

"We want to work with you in every way," a carefully groomed manager said smoothly, "but I feel obliged to tell you that if rates go too high, we will have to consider relocating our plant to a community where the business environment is more favorable.''

Kevin regarded him with disgust, translating his speech into its base components: They would move somewhere with a clean river to dump in, one that would take several years to kill. "What about pretreatment plants at your factories? If you could substantially improve the quality of what you put into our system, fewer improvements would have to be made in city treatment facilities.''

"Mr. McClain," the manager said disdainfully, "sewage is the city's problem. We were assured when we located here that all the necessary utilities were adequate and relatively inexpensive. We like Oakdale; we've been happy here, but we are in business to turn a profit. If we can no longer do that in Oakdale...."

Kevin could see the bleak realization within the committee that they were damned either way they went. They risked the wrath of residential users over increased rates or the wrath of industry threatening to take jobs away.

Gordon broke in quickly. "Obviously, we all wish we had more options with fewer undesirable side effects, but the fact is that we either come up with a viable solution within the month, or the state is going to shut Oakdale down. This committee needs something to present to the City Council at its meeting next week. My opinion is that we review the proposals from the various engineering firms who have studied our problem and recommend one to the Council." He paused, for dramatic effect, Kevin imagined. "Mrs. Miller was not bluffing, because I checked on the cities she said were under moratorium. You just think we have problems now.'' He waited for the information to seep through, then asked, "Well, what's your pleasure?''

Kevin listened to the discussion of each firm's relative merits and felt in the committee the fear of making the wrong choice. After finally reaching a consensus, they breathed a sigh of relief. The City Council would now bear the brunt of outrage over new rates. Their job was done.

As the committee drifted out, Kevin hurried back to his office to finish up his week's work. It seemed such a long time since he'd seen Becky, and she was a wonderful antidote to the poisons of long, meaningless meetings.

Becky reached the foot of the stairs to find herself face to face with the entering Kevin. He managed to get her name out before the vision of her froze him to the spot. She wore a clingy white gown accented with turquoise beading and intricately worked silver and turquoise earrings that softly brushed the side of her neck when her head moved. The stark white looked flat against the warm depth of her skin's color. The mozarkite pendant lay centered in the V of her neckline. She touched it lightly as she radiated a smile to thaw his vocal cords. "You look like an Indian angel,'' he said, touching the deep brown hair caressing her shoulders.

"Thanks, Kevin. I'm singing tonight, so I went for instant effect,'' she grinned.

"Believe me, it works,'' he leered. His face blanked for an instant. "I had something important to tell you, but you've driven it right out of my head.''

"It'll come back if it's important," she assured him. "I have had a very busy day, beginning in Gordon's office and...."

Kevin slapped his forehead. "That's it. I wanted to ask what kind of hornet's nest you stirred up today."

Becky looked at him quizzically. "I went through records at city hall, and I visited three plants, but I don't think I rang anyone's chimes unduly."

"My boss told me His Honor called him personally and instructed him to keep me away from you or anything to do with you," Kevin explained. "Doesn't that sound like ringing chimes to you?"

"It does now, but it evidently didn't at the time. We must be closer to paydirt than I thought to cause that much commotion." Becky smiled slyly.

"Why don't you relate your day's activities before I go crazy wondering what you've done?" Kevin suggested firmly.

After her account, Kevin folded his arms and frowned. "Becky, I'm not sure you should have gone charging off to those plants by yourself with no more evidence than we currently have. Price could be right about difficulties if someone wants to get nasty."

"Kevin, you sound like my mother. How can it hurt for them to know somebody may be looking over their shoulders? They're more likely to stop dumping than to put out a contract on me, wouldn't you say?" she asked serenely.

Kevin looked at her from beneath his dark scowl. "Don't underestimate these people, Becky. They have a lot at stake or they wouldn't be doing it to begin with. There are things they can do besides inflicting physical violence on you, you know."

"Kevin, I appreciate your concern, but quit worrying about me. Come on into the club, and I'll dedicate the first set to you," she coaxed smoothly, taking his arm and starting down the hall. "Any special requests I can fill?"

"Just one, Becky," he said, stopping to face her with pleading in his troubled eyes. "Please don't take all this so lightly. I can assure you that our adversary doesn't."

Becky kissed him warmly. "You're a worrywart, Kevin, and I'm a big girl who can look out for herself if push comes to shove...and I don't think it will. Besides, we're finally getting some action. Now, think of a song you want to hear," she urged as she steered him toward the club.

Becky dropped Kevin off at a table and walked toward the trio already playing at the front of the room. He ordered a beer and settled down to some serious worrying. He was convinced Becky had no idea what she was dealing with. A cornered animal could be an unpredictably dangerous animal. He knew how important it was to Becky to get to the bottom of this thing, but he knew also she was new to the local politics of power and profit. That naiveté was a source of anxiety to Kevin, but there seemed to be nothing he could do to protect Becky. She didn't want protection, and the city job tied his hands even further. All he could do was to stay as close as possible, to give her the most refined ammunition he could muster, and to keep cautioning her along the way. Becky was very special to him, and that fact magnified in Kevin's eyes the risks she took.

Becky flashed a dazzling smile at Kevin as the piano set up a musical frame for her to step into. At the first note of her tawny golden voice, Kevin felt waves of excitement ripple through his torso. The mellow piano and the husky voice flew like mating birds, taking with them the ears and hearts of their listeners. Not so much as the tinkle of an ice cube in a glass could be heard as the magic of her music enchanted them like flies caught in amber.

Becky's love song poured over Kevin like molten gold; beauty, pleasure, and the sweet pain that attends those emotions. The music hovered around his heart like a tentative knock at a closed door. When she sang, Becky had the wonderful quality of immediacy, of authentic feeling clothed in harmony and words, of being at the dead center of every moment as it lived. Suddenly Kevin wanted Becky all to himself. He didn't want to share her with the world, with an environmental crusade, or even with her business. He wanted to hold her, to love and cherish her uniqueness with everything he had to offer. He felt his entire being threatened with the flood of emotion rushing to open that door at which she tapped so gently. Just when he realized the tightness in his chest came from suspended breathing, the last note fell like the downy reminder of a lark's flight, leaving him feeling strangely bereft.

Kevin managed to sit through the first set without doing anything outrageous, but only by sheer force of his disciplined will. He fervently prayed for the day he would be free to be as lovingly outrageous with her as he liked.

Becky sang her songs as if everyone had left Kevin and her alone in the room. She felt so free when she sang, using someone else's words to say the lovely, poetic, sensual things she couldn't say without feeling a little silly. She wanted him to feel her hands on his heart, her lips on his body, her soul in his mind, and she sang to him of these very private things in this very public place. She could feel the fire in her own veins reaching out to ignite his pulsing response. By the end of the first set, she regretted having promised to sing all evening. What she wanted more than anything was to soar with Kevin to the top of their mutual passion, to glide on the magical music to a place removed from all the petty problems of the world. But what she did was finish the set and walk calmly back to Kevin's table.

She placed her cool hand in his warm grasp, and for a moment, they sat without speaking, letting the tides flow and mingle and finally ebb away, their power reserved for another time and place.

"I didn't know people could make love in such a public place," Kevin finally said, his voice husky and hushed, "but that was the closest I've ever come at that distance." He kissed her hand. "Do you love me as much as I love you?"

She smiled at his question. "How can I answer without knowing how much you love me?" She stroked the tablecloth with one fingernail. "I love you more than I've ever loved any man, Kevin, perhaps more than I thought I could love a man."

"And you ain't seen nothin' yet," he whispered intensely, his heart filling his veins with a rush of life as the door burst open, compounding the heat of desire with the light of promise.

Clad in jeans, chambray shirt, and hiking boots, her ample tresses confined under a red bandanna scarf,

Becky sat under the big white oak tree drinking coffee and waiting for Kevin. She was looking forward to a day of hiking around in the woods with him, even if the purpose of their outing wasn't purely pleasure. Just after nine o'clock he arrived and joined her for a quick cup.

"I figured we might not be back by lunchtime," Becky said, indicating a knapsack on the ground beside her, "so I packed some sandwiches."

"Good thinking," Kevin approved, hefting a large backpack from his car.

Becky regarded the big pack in amazement. "We're not going to be gone that long, are we?"

Kevin chuckled. "This is not clean underwear, my dear; it's a portable lab with testing equipment, bottles, bags, and various sample-collection paraphernalia." He shrugged it onto his broad shoulders and buckled the waist belt securely.

"I think I'd rather carry sandwiches," Becky retorted, slipping her arms through the straps of her small knapsack. "No wonder all those mad scientists in the late movies needed bearers. I think this little safari is more my speed. The creek is over there." She pointed across the parking area to where woods began.

They walked to the edge of the cleared land where the woods started its descent to the foot of the hill and the bed of a lazy creek. Up the stream from where they stood, they could hear a swift riffle and below them the creek widened for a small pool before virtually disappearing from sight. "Pretty typical for a stream in this type of soil," Kevin commented. "Spends as much of its length underground as it does on top. My guess is

1. How do you rate _____
   (Please print book TITLE)

   1.6 ☐ excellent   .4 ☐ good   .2 ☐ not so good
   .5 ☐ very good   .3 ☐ fair   .1 ☐ poor

2. How likely are you to purchase another book:
   in this *series*?   by this *author*?
   2.1 ☐ definitely would purchase   3.1 ☐ definitely would purchase
   .2 ☐ probably would puchase   .2 ☐ probably would puchase
   .3 ☐ probably would not purchase   .3 ☐ probably would not purchase
   .4 ☐ definitely would not purchase   .4 ☐ definitely would not purchase

   A123

3. How does this book compare with similar books you usually read?
   4.1 ☐ far better than others   .2 ☐ better than others   .3 ☐ about the
   .4 ☐ not as good   .5 ☐ definitely not as good   same

4. Please check the statements you feel best describe this book.
   5. ☐ Easy to read   6. ☐ Too much violence/anger
   7. ☐ Realistic conflict   8. ☐ Wholesome/not too sexy
   9. ☐ Too sexy   10. ☐ Interesting characters
   11. ☐ Original plot   12. ☐ Especially romantic
   13. ☐ Not enough humor   14. ☐ Difficult to read
   15. ☐ Didn't like the subject   16. ☐ Good humor in story
   17. ☐ Too predictable   18. ☐ Not enough description of setting
   19. ☐ Believable characters   20. ☐ Fast paced
   21. ☐ Couldn't put the book down   22. ☐ Heroine too juvenile/weak/silly
   23. ☐ Made me feel good   24. ☐ Too many foreign/unfamiliar words
   25. ☐ Hero too dominating   26. ☐ Too wholesome/not sexy enough
   27. ☐ Not enough romance   28. ☐ Liked the setting
   29. ☐ Ideal hero   30. ☐ Heroine too independent
   31. ☐ Slow moving   32. ☐ Unrealistic conflict
   33. ☐ Not enough suspense   34. ☐ Sensuous/not too sexy
   35. ☐ Liked the subject   36. ☐ Too much description of setting

5. What *most* prompted you to buy this book?
   37. ☐ Read others in series   38. ☐ Title   39. ☐ Cover art
   40. ☐ Friend's recommendation 41. ☐ Author   42. ☐ In-store display
   43. ☐ TV, radio or magazine ad 44. ☐ Price   45. ☐ Story outline
   46. ☐ Ad inside other books   47. ☐ Other _____ (please specify)

6. Please indicate how many romance paperbacks you read in a month.
   48.1 ☐ 1 to 4   .2 ☐ 5 to 10   .3 ☐ 11 to 15   .4 ☐ more than 15

7. Please indicate your sex and age group.
   49.1 ☐ Male   50.1 ☐ under 15   .3 ☐ 25-34   .5 ☐ 50-64
   .2 ☐ Female   .2 ☐ 15-24   .4 ☐ 35-49   .6 ☐ 65 or older

8. Have you any additional comments about this book?
   _____ (51)
   _____ (53)

Thank you for completing and returning this questionnaire.
Printed in USA

NAME _____
ADDRESS _____

(Please Print)

CITY _____
ZIP CODE _____

BUSINESS REPLY MAIL

FIRST CLASS   PERMIT NO. 70   TEMPE, AZ.

POSTAGE WILL BE PAID BY ADDRESSEE

NATIONAL READER SURVEYS

2504 West Southern Avenue
Tempe, AZ   85282

that the stuff is coming down the creek, going underground with the water, straight to a fault that opens
into your pond.''

''Sounds reasonable to me,'' Becky agreed. ''What
are we supposed to be looking for?''

''Anything that looks out of place: wood, leaves,
even mud that's a little too dark or scummy, any areas
of stagnant water.'' He peered upstream. ''Have you
been very far up the creek?''

''Not since I was a kid. Best I remember, it runs
pretty fast a mile or so up from here, but it begins to
fizzle out by the time it gets here.''

''Just going underground. Okay, you take this side
and I'll take the other. At least there's walking room
around the creek.'' He hopped across the narrow chan-
nel and started walking slowly, bent at the hips to scan
the ground as he moved over it.

Becky followed suit. ''What will you do with these
samples?''

''If we find anything interesting, I'll run a chromatograph. If it matches the samples from your place, we'll
know it came through here.''

''It is a safari of sorts, isn't it?'' Becky flashed a smile
across the creek before settling back to her close scrutiny.

They walked without speaking, each intent on the
search, their peripheral senses enjoying the fine summer day. Occasionally Kevin stooped to examine a leaf
or piece of dead wood, less frequently putting a sample
in a plastic bag from his pack. Becky hadn't seen anything suspicious yet, and she began to worry about
missing something. Her next footfall brought her to a

pocket scooped into the bank where water sat stagnant, separated from the stream and trapped. Becky noticed the scum on the surface wasn't the usual mossy green but much darker. Leaves floating on it were slimy and much too dark. "Kevin, come look at this."

He stepped across the creek to join her. He stuck his thumb and forefinger into the scum and rubbed them together. "Well, it's certainly some sort of oily substance. We'd better take some samples." He unfastened the pack and hoisted it to the ground. From one compartment, he retrieved a plastic bottle into which he carefully dipped the foul water and a plastic bag for some of the leaves. With a marker from his shirt pocket, he labeled the bottle and the bag with a number one. Next, he took from another compartment some surveyer's flags, stuck the stiff wire into the ground beside the puddle and wrote the same number on the orange plastic flag.

Becky watched his methodical procedure with interest. "How come you didn't flag any of the other places you picked up samples?" she inquired curiously.

"I don't think they're likely to be of any use to us. This looks promising," he explained, hefting the pack into place again. "We should find even more as we go upstream. How far from here to any industrial areas?"

Becky frowned. "I don't know for sure. Maybe two or three miles, as the crow flies. Would it travel that far?"

"Easily," Kevin assured her grimly. "Let's keep moving."

For another hour they combed both sides of the creek without finding anything of interest. When the creek narrowed to a fast-running ribbon, bringing them nearly shoulder to shoulder, Kevin flexed his shoulders against the load he was carrying. "My back says it's time to take a break."

"My stomach concurs," Becky said. "This is a pretty nice place for a picnic." The ground sloped up steeply to a grassy bank under a spreading sycamore tree. They clambered up quickly, and Kevin propped his pack against the tree.

"It's so pretty out here," he commented, dropping onto the grass. "It's really criminal for somebody to crud up a place like this with industrial waste."

Becky handed him a brown paper bag, keeping another for herself. He pulled out two plastic-wrapped sandwiches and a small plastic bag of fresh blueberries. Kevin grinned in surprise. "Where did you get these?"

"They're grown locally, and we buy them by the flat to make fancy desserts at the restaurant. You'll find the sandwiches to be thoroughly mundane: one is provolone cheese, the other peanut butter, but I thought they'd travel well." She reached into the pack for a plastic bottle. "Considering our errand, I thought bringing water was the better part of valor." She grinned, setting it between them on the grass.

Kevin laughed, unwrapping his sandwich. They consumed the lunch with dispatch, washing it down with the bottled water, and lay back on the soft grass to rest before continuing.

"This may be detective work," Becky observed from her prone position, "but it's pretty dull compared to Mike Hammer or Perry Mason, you'll have to admit."

Kevin looked over at her indignantly. "I'll have to

admit no such thing. You just watch too much TV. I think it's pretty exciting stuff.''

"Only a scientist could say that and mean it," she remarked dubiously.

"If excitement is what you crave," he said, raising up on one elbow to look down at her, "I can do something about that." The mischievous grin transformed into a coaxing kiss. Becky's arms slipped around Kevin's neck like homing pigeons as she responded to him.

"This is more fun than bottling yukky water," Becky giggled, "but we won't get a matched set of chromatograms this way."

"Spoken like a true scientist," Kevin groaned. "I guess we'd better get moving again."

They donned their packs and continued upstream, flagging two more sites after tucking samples safely away in Kevin's pack. Becky found she was moving more slowly, her leg muscles unaccustomed to so much exercise in one day. As she stepped into the edge of the stream to avoid a low-hanging branch, her boot slipped and she landed on her bottom in the cold, racing water.

At the splash Kevin turned quickly. His lips twitched with the effort to maintain their sober aspect. "Becky, if you want to rest, all you have to do is say so and I'll stop."

Throwing him a look designed to fry him, Becky started to get to her feet, only to slip again, this time landing on her back in the shallow water. Kevin slipped off his pack and set it on the bank quickly. "Boy, I'm glad you waited until after lunch to do this," he said as he walked toward her. "I can't stand soggy sandwiches."

"Here I lie in contaminated water, no doubt picking up some toxic substance from which I will waste away in agony, and all you can do is make snide remarks," she fumed at him. "Help me up."

"I'll help you up, but don't worry about the water. Most of the time it isn't contaminated anyway," he explained calmly, reaching his hand out to her.

"In that case," she said, yanking him abruptly, "why don't you join me?" Before he could regain his balance, he found himself sitting beside her.

"Now who's going to help me up so I can help you up?" Kevin asked wryly.

"It's every woman for herself," Becky giggled, hoisting herself from the water, using Kevin as support. Before she could escape, he pulled her across his lap and kissed her soundly. With a swat to her wet rear, he pushed her to her feet again and followed her out of the water.

"What an ignominious ending to a scientific expedition," he moaned, regarding his soaked clothes ruefully.

"Have we gone far enough upstream?" Becky asked, wringing water from her shirttail.

"Hard to tell, but I think we'll call it a day anyway." He reached for the pack. "I'll run these samples, and if I find what we're looking for, we'll go on upstream next time and keep sampling until we don't find anything. That will pinpoint an area to search for the outlet."

As they started back, Kevin looked at Becky solemnly. "Exactly what do you intend doing about my wet clothes, for which I hold you personally responsible?"

She shrugged blithely. "I suppose you could throw them in my dryer, but you'd have to stay in bed until they were done."

"Is that an invitation?" he leered hopefully with a sidelong glance at the firm, high breasts to which Becky's wet shirt clung.

"I have dry clothes to change into," she teased, evading his question, "but a blanket is the only thing I have that would fit you."

He reached over to tweak one breast gently. "Keep walking and save your strength, then."

They walked hand in hand back to the restaurant, their comfortable silence a satisfying communion. Becky was continually amazed at the way they seemed to be fitting themselves to each other. She could hardly remember the time before knowing him, and she had to remind herself it was a very few weeks since the first fish kill. But they were making progress on that front, too, she felt confident. They were on their way to a solution and, she hoped, a happy ending for everybody.

Chapter Eight

"A perfect match," Kevin crowed. His phone call got Becky out of bed Monday morning to report the chromatograms of the creek samples matched perfectly with the samples from the fish pond the night of the kill. "Looks like we're finally getting enough ammunition to think about going to the authorities. We'll have to go back to the creek and follow it farther upstream. Want to do it this week or wait for the weekend?"

"Are you kidding? I want to go right now."

"Not so fast. I have this little matter of school and a job to keep up with, Becky. How about tomorrow afternoon?"

"That's good. Meanwhile, I'll visit the other two plants on my list and call Pollution Control. Looks like they'll have to listen now, doesn't it?"

Kevin didn't sound convinced. "Well, we can always hope. See you tomorrow."

Becky depressed the receiver button long enough to reactivate the dial tone. She dialed the now-familiar number for Pollution Control and asked for the inspector she'd talked with before. "Good morning, Mr.

Gaines. This is Becky Sherman. You remember the Oakdale trout kill?''

"What can I do for you, Ms Sherman?" the voice asked evenly.

She briefly outlined what she and Kevin had done and the results of his lab tests. "The chromatograms are a perfect match, Mr. Gaines. Is that enough for you to start an investigation?"

"It's certainly enough for us to look at your results, Ms Sherman, but I've reviewed your case and find all our tests came up negative. We still don't like to start investigations on anyone's data but our own, you know."

"Listen, Mr. Gaines," Becky flared, her excitement hardening to anger, "the man who took the samples and did the testing is with the university. Surely you're not implying the university lab is in some sort of conspiracy with me to malign some poor innocent factory."

"Ms Sherman, I'm not implying anything. This is nothing personal, as I've told you. Our policies are designed to prevent our jumping on somebody else's white charger and getting thrown."

"You can get thrown off a jackass, too," Becky snapped.

After a second of silence, Gaines spoke in a carefully controlled tone. "Tell you what, Ms Sherman, I'll send a man up to get some samples from the creek. He can also look at the lab reports from the university, but he can't get there before Thursday at the earliest. We're working a train spill in the eastern part of the state, and it's taking everyone we can pull in. I'll send you some-

one as soon as I can get him freed up. Okay?'' he ended
wearily.

"Okay. And while I'm waiting, I'll get you some more
hard evidence. Mr. Gaines, I intend to keep trying until I
can hand you something you can't refuse to accept.''

"You'll be hearing from us by the end of the week,
Ms Sherman.'' He broke the connection without further formality.

Becky glared impotently at the dead receiver. What
did he want? Eyewitnesses? No, he'd think they were
lying, too. She slammed it down, enraged by the unsatisfactory response she always got from the state. "And
that's supposed to be the environment's first line of defense?'' she sneered. "Abandon hope, Mother Earth!''

She dressed quickly, deciding she might as well visit
her two factories. Becky liked to finish lists in an or-
derly fashion, and she might stumble across something
significant, which she was unlikely to do sitting at
home fuming.

Both plant managers were cooperative, showing her
their records of waste disposal. They both believed a
waste hauler was the likely culprit, unless someone was
refusing to admit to an accidental spill, which would be
pretty shortsighted. Becky crossed the last two names
off, leaving the second and third plants she'd visited
and anonymous waste haulers as her prime suspects.
Deciding Gordon Yates should be able to help her
track down local waste haulers, she headed for city hall.

"Nice tie, Gordon,'' she greeted the tall young man
behind the piled-up desk. When he looked up, surprise
on his face, she relented. "Just kidding, Gordon. It's
awful.''

"You had me scared for a minute." He grinned. "Been out poking sticks into hornets' nests this morning?"

"Oh Lord, you, too?" she groaned. "What are you talking about, Gordon?"

"Shame on you, out harrassing our local industrialists, accusing them of all sorts of terrible things." He shook his head. "Don't think I haven't heard about it, too."

"Gordon, all I did was visit five plants who use the kind of oils we're looking for," she protested.

"Doesn't take much to stampede a frightened animal," he commented wryly. "The general impression is that you're a real troublemaker and probably, if you'll pardon the language, some sort of environmentalist or feminist in league with Janice Miller to destroy the number-one growth area in the whole state."

"They may not be far from the mark, but they're a whole lot responsible for it," Becky said, eyes snapping. She related her interviews with Pollution Control and the plant managers. "They seem very anxious to lay it at the feet of the waste haulers, so I figured I might as well check them out, too. Where do I get a list of waste haulers working in this area?"

Gordon expelled his breath with a whoosh. "You think some of the industries have been uncooperative; wait until you start trying to track waste haulers down. They don't have to be registered with the Environmental Protection Agency unless they're hauling hazardous wastes. I think they're all supposed to register with Pollution Control, so you might call the state again. We don't have many operating in this area, so I don't know a whole lot about them...fortunately."

"Easy for you to say. Any more helpful suggestions?"

"Yeah." He grinned widely. "Keep pokin' and stirrin' out there. It's good for 'em."

Becky waved as she opened his door to leave. As she passed the secretary, she smiled. "I don't think that tie is so bad, do you?" she said loudly and kept walking.

"Hello again, Mr. Gaines," Becky said pleasantly. "Do you have a list of all the industrial waste haulers operating in this area?"

"If they're hauling hazardous wastes, we have a record of what was picked up and where it was taken, but no one in your area is producing hazardous wastes."

"What about people who haul wastes not classified as hazardous?"

"We don't keep up with that kind of hauler. Waste of that type is usually dumped in landfills."

"Or by the side of a country road?" Becky couldn't resist asking pointedly.

"There are undoubtedly a few 'midnight dumpers' in this state, but I assure you it's not a widespread or serious problem for us."

"Is there any way I could track down these people?"

"Other than asking the industry itself whom they use, I don't know. We can require that industry to show us their disposal records, if we have a solid identification of the substance and reason to track it to them. I tend to doubt the waste hauler theory, Ms Sherman."

"Well, since you don't seem to have any better ideas, I'll see what I can do with it, Mr. Gaines. You'll be hearing from me again," she assured him before hanging up. Becky had no real idea what she was going to do about it, however. She had jotted down names from the records she saw at the cooperative plants, but she knew she was probably most interested in United Industries, and they weren't going to give her the time of day.

Momentarily discouraged with the whole thing, she tried to call Kevin for consultation or commiseration, whichever he could offer. He wasn't at any of the numbers she tried, so she gave up and decided to work on the restaurant's books, a chore she'd sadly neglected since everything started. It would pass the time, as well as get her mind off her helplessness.

Afternoon crept into evening, and business at the restaurant was too slow to distract Becky from her growing gloom. When Kevin appeared, she greeted him with faint enthusiasm.

"Becky, what's the matter? I don't think I've ever seen you so glum." He kissed her on the cheek and slipped his arm around her waist. "Come tell me what's happened," he urged softly, leading her to their table.

"Nothing has happened," she sighed, "and that's the problem, Kevin. I feel like I'm trying to walk through a sea of half-set Jell-O. I don't feel like we're getting anywhere at all, and I'm running out of ideas fast."

Out of nowhere Sheila quietly appeared with two glasses and a bottle of sparkling wine, deposited them near Kevin's elbow, and kept walking. He shot her a smile of thanks and poured a glass for Becky, then for himself. "Drink this. You'll feel better," he ordered with a slight smile. "Becky, you're doing just fine, but don't be in such a hurry. Things like this take a lot of time and patience."

"I'm rapidly running out of time and patience," she snapped sullenly, accepting the glass.

"I know it's hard when you can't see any progress." He sipped at his drink. "Believe me, that Jell-O is quivering around the edges." He smiled crookedly.

"It is?" she asked, her curiosity overcoming her melancholy. "How do you know?"

"Because I spent some time in the boss's office this afternoon, summoned there to listen to a lecture about keeping my academic interests out of my city job. You see, I've been going through some of Water and Sewer's records to see who is at full capacity on what they're running through the system. I also mentioned at a committee meeting that I was helping you with some testing."

"Kevin...." Becky's face betrayed her alarm.

"I was instructed to stick to items that were in my job description, which that certainly wasn't. I was also told very cleary that if I couldn't interest myself in doing what I was hired to do, they could probably find someone who would be."

"Oh, Kevin, you can't jeopardize your job over this," Becky wailed.

"Don't you see what that means, Becky? That means somebody is worried enough to be leaning on the mayor to lean on me. The Jell-O is quivering like hell out there somewhere."

"But how would you pay for school if...."

"I told you once before I was looking for a job when I found this one," he stated firmly. "I've played it pretty conservative to this point, but I'm beginning to get mad. I don't like the smell of cover-up I'm getting down there, and I don't like being threatened. I won't worry about it if you won't.'' He squeezed her hand. ''Besides, you said I could always come bone trout for you if I got fired.''

She smiled wanly. ''With no more business than we have tonight, I couldn't buy your books.''

''I'll spend more time in the library, so don't worry about it.''

''I really can't let you risk your job, Kevin. After all this is our problem, not yours,'' she insisted.

He raised the outer corners of his eyebrows in an impatient expression. ''What does it take to convince you I regard your problems as mine? I thought we were in this together to the bitter end. Now, what happened today to get you down so low?''

''I talked to Pollution Control twice for openers,'' she noted dryly. ''That's enough to ruin anyone's day, isn't it? I can't even find out if there are any waste haulers in this part of the state, much less who they are. They're like will-o'-the-wisps flickering in the swamp.''

After her narrative, Kevin shook his head in wonder. ''I'm not surprised you're discouraged, Becky, but we really are several steps ahead of where we were this time last week, aren't we?''

''I guess so,'' she admitted grudgingly, ''but it seems we're the only people who are mad about what's happening.''

''Were you mad...or even informed...before your fish died?'' he chided her gently. ''They're no better or worse than you were, Becky. They don't know what's going on, and they've never had any reason to care."

"High time they did, then," she said flatly. "I think I'll go to the City Council meeting tomorrow night and do a little educational project...see if I can't stir up some righteous indignation."

"Have you really thought that through?" Kevin asked, folding his arms and frowning.

"Look around you. How can our business be hurt anymore than it is? Dad has some good friends on the Council. I've already talked to some of them, and I think they would be willing to get the city to investigate on what we have now. Kevin, I'm at a standstill. I can't barge into a private industry and demand to see anybody's records, but the city can." She leaned across the table, reaching for his approval.

Kevin searched her animated face, his blue eyes clouded. "I wish you'd talk to your father and give it some more thought. In my opinion, it's not the thing to do at this point."

"It's at least something to do besides sitting on my hands, endlessly waiting for someone else to solve my problem. If nothing else, I can let them know what's going on."

"What we think is going on," Kevin corrected her. "Our proof is still incomplete, Becky. I know you're going to do what you think you have to do, so I won't say any more about it. I'll be here right after noon tomorrow to finish the sampling and run the tests as quickly as I can. I don't think I can have anything in time for the meeting though." He changed the subject, seeing her depression beginning to fade at the prospect of something to be done, contenting himself with the hope she would rethink her impulsive decision before the meeting. His extensive experience with the City Council led him to fear her plan would backfire in her lovely face.

After Kevin and Becky returned from their second trek up the creek for samples, Becky told her father about her determination to confront the City Council with what they already knew, even if their latest samples wouldn't be processed yet. Like Kevin, Gene didn't think much of Becky's plan to go, but he reluctantly agreed to accompany her if she was so set on it.

When they arrived at city hall, they were surprised to see Kevin waiting for them outside the meeting room. "Kevin, your job..." Becky began.

"For the record, I think you're making a mistake, but if you insist on going through with it, I'll stay with you. You might need an expert witness." He hushed her as they entered the room.

They wouldn't be on the regular agenda, but one of Gene's friends had promised Becky he would bring it up under New Business, Other. As they sat patiently through the routine business of the Council, Becky recognized only three of the seven Council members. Oakdale had grown so fast in recent years, the newcomers were beginning to seriously outnumber the natives like Gene and Frances. Even though she grew up in Oakdale, Becky recognized few people in the room. A vague unease formed in her chest.

When her name was called, Becky related as quickly and concisely as possible the events of recent weeks, ending with a request for help. "I would like to ask the city to check the records of five area industries to see if they can help us find the source of this pollution."

A meticulously groomed man about Kevin's age spoke up when she had finished. "Mr. Mayor, I fail to see what any of this really has to do with the city. I'm sure we're sympathetic with Ms Sherman's plight, but her farm is outside the city limits. By her own admission, she doesn't believe the problem to be caused by city waste, so it seems to me the city is out of it all around. It's obviously a matter for the State Pollution Control Agency."

Several councilmen nodded in agreement. One of Gene's friends quickly asked Becky to be more precise in clarifying what she wanted from the city. Feeling her support slipping away, Becky took a deep breath. "The city knows exactly what is going into the sewer system from every plant, and those records have been made available to me. But the city can request from industry an accounting of any wastes handled in some other way. You can find out who is hauling this waste and where it's being dumped. All I'm asking is for you to check out what's being done. It was dumped on us last time, but it might be inside city limits next time. If illegal dumping is going on, it's certainly in your best interests to know about it and help put a stop to it."

The opposing councilman spoke again. "Ms Sherman, we've worked hard to bring industrial jobs to this town, and we've screened the industries very carefully. We have some of the best plants here you'll find anywhere, and I think you do them a disservice by wanting us to play gestapo with them. I for one would be opposed to doing anything that implied we believed they were engaged in illegal or unethical activity. In case you haven't heard, the most important item on our agenda tonight is trying to decide where we're going to get the millions of dollars we need for a new waste treatment plant the state is forcing on us. One of our options is to raise industrial rates to finance the new plant. If we do that, we face losing those industries and the jobs they provide. Without industry Oakdale could revert to the one-horse town it was twenty years ago. It seems to me the last thing we need to do is compound our problems by choosing to harass these industries further without better cause. I move we deny this request, Mr. Mayor."

After a quick second, the motion was passed by a vote of four to three, and the regular agenda proceeded. Kevin ushered the stunned Becky and Gene out of the room quickly. "I think this town was better with just one horse's behind in it," Gene muttered as they left. "This wouldn't have happened even ten years ago, but seems like everybody's crazy for progress at any price."

"Your friends stuck, Gene, they were just outnumbered," Kevin reminded the older man. "Three friends are better than none, I always say."

"Yeah, I guess so," Gene grinned, shaking his head. Becky knew Gene was upset by this unavoidable evidence of the change in Oakdale. No longer the small friendly town he knew and loved, it was being flooded with outsiders who wanted to build another city like the one they left.

"Are you okay?" Kevin squeezed Becky's shoulders. At her nod, he veered toward his own car. "I'll call you in the morning. The chromatograms should be done by then."

Driving home, Becky tried to cheer Gene up. "So who needs them anyway? Agatha Christie's detectives never need help from the village council, do they?"

Gene chuckled, his even dispostion working to blot up the disappointment he felt, and began talking about needing to move the fast-growing fingerlings again soon.

Becky listened with one ear, but she couldn't be quite as philosophical about it as her father could. She was outraged at the Council's action and absolutely furious with the man who railroaded it through. She would have to find out more about him, like whose payroll he was on. She made a mental note to have Kevin ask Gordon about him.

Unable to face her mother's "I won't say I told you so but I did" face, Becky dropped Gene off. Only then, in solitude, did she begin to wonder if she made it clear enough that the pollution had consumed the trout's oxygen, that there was nothing wrong with Rainbow Ribbon fish. Business was slow enough as it was without the councilmen going home to spread some misunderstanding about the fish she served in her restaurant.

In bed that night, Becky reviewed everything they had done to date and tried to plan her next step. She had to produce incontrovertible evidence before anyone would do anything. She needed something nobody could argue with, but she believed there must be some way other than Kevin's patient, plodding accumulation of damning details. Tomorrow she would head back up the creek to look for the source of the dumping. There had to be a pipe or some opening to indicate where the substance entered the stream. If she could find that, get matching samples, it would be a simple matter to follow the pipe to the sludge pond or whatever.

As she dozed off, Becky knew it wouldn't be quite as simple as all that, but it was another something she could do while Kevin proceeded in his scientific but agonizingly slow amassing of data.

Douglas Price circulated among the throng gathered for his unusual cocktail party. He hardly ever enterained during the work week, but he thought it would be more convenient for the councilmen to come straight from their meeting. He wanted to show his gratitude for the mayor's support and he wanted to start his little rumor in fertile and influential ears.

Passing a group of his colleagues' wives, he heard one of them say, "I know it's hard to believe, and Mrs. Price said she was sure there was nothing to it, but if their fish are dying like flies, I don't think we'll eat there any more."

"Such a nice place, too," another woman clucked. "What a shame."

Price smiled and sipped at his martini. By the time it reached the outer branches of the grapevine, everybody would know somebody who got sick eating at Rainbow's End. The business community was tightly knit, and the word would travel quickly. That little troublemaker would have her thoughts too full of empty tables to meddle in his business. He patted the mayor on the shoulder, offered the helpful councilman another drink, and began to relax for the first time in a week.

Chapter Nine

"Bingo!" Kevin said gleefully as soon as Becky picked up the phone, not even waiting for a greeting.

"Good morning, Kevin. You said 'bingo'?"

"Good morning, and yes, I did. We have a run, Becky. The samples test out to the next-to-the-last flag. That means we have the area isolated."

"Kevin, that's terrific." Becky began to gear up with excitement. "Now we look for a pipe or some sort of outlet, right?"

"Right. Or maybe tire marks where a truck backed down to the creek or near enough for a hose to reach."

"I'll get started as soon as I dress," she said briskly. "I haven't had breakfast yet, but it won't...."

"Hold your horses," Kevin interrupted her. "My boss seems intent on keeping me very busy this week. I'm scheduled to spend the rest of the week staking out a new street with a survey crew. I won't have time to get out until the weekend."

"That's okay. I can take a look today, and let you know if I find anything."

Kevin met her suggestion with a silent pause. "Becky, I'd rather you didn't go alone."

"Kevin," she said in surprise, "I'll know a pipe when I see one. I don't need you for that."

"That's not what I mean, and you know it," he chided her.

"Kevin, I've been up and down that creek a hundred times. What are you worried about?"

"I hate to bring up age, but it's been several years since you spent much time on that creek, Becky, and things are different now."

"Kevin, all I'm going to do is check the area between the last two flags for anything obviously out of the ordinary. I won't disturb anything that might be evidence, I'll go in broad daylight, and I'll be careful." She paused, slightly annoyed at what she considered his overprotective attitude. "Kevin, I'm perfectly capable of doing this little errand. Why wait another three or four days until you're free?"

He sighed resignedly. "I'd just prefer you waited for me, that's all."

"It seems waiting is all I've been doing since this thing started," Becky said impatiently. "I'm tired of waiting for somebody else to do something, especially when it's something like this I can do myself." She didn't want to sound harsh, but she wasn't going to let him dissuade her. "Why don't you come by tonight for a report? That's more fun than phones."

"That's for sure," he agreed, still uneasy about Becky's determination to proceed alone. "Becky, be careful, will you?"

"Of course, I will. Oh, would you ask Gordon who that councilman is? You know, the one who gave us so much trouble at the meeting?"

"I'll ask him. See you tonight."

"Bye." As she replaced the receiver, she felt real ambivalence about Kevin's trying to get her to wait for him. She knew he was concerned about her safety, and she appreciated that, but she was used to doing things her own way. Being protected by a man might have appeal as an abstract concept, but she wasn't accustomed to it in reality. Becky had managed to take care of herself for a number of years without a man's assistance. Still, it was nice to know he cared that much about her. Oh well, time to sort all that out later.

Quickly dressing in jeans, boots, and a long-sleeved shirt to protect her arms against brush, Becky struck out northeast over the hill, planning to hit the creek farther upstream than last time. She descended not quite on target, still some way from her search area and out of breath from haste. She paused a moment to reconnoiter before proceeding.

The morning was warm, and little air stirred in the creek bottom. The only sounds were insects buzzing, the gurgling of water hurrying by, and Becky's hasty progress over snapping twigs and rustling grass. She quickly located the next-to-last flag they planted and began a careful search up the south side of the creek, ranging as far as fifty feet from the stream bed, thinking someone could have backed a truck close enough to use a hose. Most of this section of the creek was scrub trees and brush, and Becky didn't really think a truck of any size could be brought in without leaving obvious signs. There were places she doubted a truck could negotiate at all.

She reached the last flag, having found nothing to

arouse her suspicion, and turned to return down the
north side of the creek. Becky searched even more
carefully, but she soon found herself back at her starting place...with nothing to show for her efforts. She
wiped her sleeve across her forehead to remove the
sweat beginning to trickle into her eyes and looked
back the way she had come. It had to be there. How was
she missing it? She sat beside the creek for a minute,
splashed some of the clear, cold water on her face and
caught her breath. The sultry air seemed to be consum-
ing her oxygen supply.

Suddenly there was a sound of brush snapping under
someone's foot, and Becky's heart mobilized her body
for flight. She sat still, her pulse pounding, wondering
if Kevin had been right after all. Slowly she turned to
look in the direction of the sound. Two solemn brown
eyes regarded her for a moment before the cow
lowered her head to drink from the creek. "Damned
old hussy," Becky hissed as her pent breath exploded
with relief. As soon as the adrenaline ebbed sufficiently
for her to stand, Becky began methodically retracing
her former route.

This time she moved every bush and looked under
every tree root, thinking her first examination had simply been too rushed. When she came full circle, she
admitted failure. In spite of her meticulous efforts,
there was nothing to be found. Kevin had been so sure,
she didn't understand why she couldn't find anything.
Maybe she misunderstood his directions to the search
area. Maybe it was farther upstream.

Until midafternoon Becky drove herself with the
conviction she must be missing something she knew

had to be there. After she couldn't remember how many trips over the same ground, she gave up, sitting dejectedly on the bank to rest a moment before starting the long trek home. She had been so sure she would find something, so sure she could do it without Kevin's help. As she stared into the bubbling water, wishing it could talk, a cracking twig snapped her head around to see a man leaning against a tree not ten feet from where she sat. A coarse, heavily built man in his fifties, obviously used to hard physical labor, he watched her with an unpleasant grin. The patch over one shirt pocket of his uniform read UNITED, the other CHARLEY. Becky quickly scrambled to her feet, feeling like a rabbit in a trap.

"Well, now, I wonder what a pretty young lady like you would be doin' wanderin' around in these woods all by herself?" he said softly.

"I'm just...just out for a walk," Becky improvised, hoping he was dumber than he looked, "and I'm not alone." She smiled brightly. "My friend and I split up to look for samples, and"—she glanced quickly at her watch—"oh, dear, it's time for us to rendezvous right now. I'd better be going, or he'll come looking for me."

Charley laughed, a nasal, braying denial of her assertion. "Nice try, but I know you're lyin', girl. I was up the hill workin' and heard all your splashin' around, so I came down to check it out. I been watchin' you for quite a while." He hefted his bulk off the tree and started walking toward her. "What exactly are you doin' here, anyway?"

Becky fought down her growing panic. "I'm a biologist. I study the kind of waterbugs that live in running water," she said with as much poise as she could muster, her blood pounding like thunder in her ears. "I was looking for specimens of a particular kind."

"Waterbugs, huh?" Charley snorted his disbelief and advanced another few steps until he stood close enough for her to see the veins in his ruddy face. "This is private property, Miss Biologist, and the waterbugs belong to us, along with everything else. The boss don't much like people sneakin' around behind our backs." He stepped so close Becky shrank a half step to avoid physical contact, but she couldn't avoid the low, suggestive growl reaching for her. "Even a pretty little thing like you could come to harm snoopin' around on private property, out here where nobody could even hear you holler," he added pointedly, "and we sure wouldn't want to take responsibility for a terrible thing like that." A stubby finger tugged at a lock of hair tumbling from under Becky's bandanna. "And you are a pretty little thing, ain't you?"

Becky wanted to scream and run, but she controlled her fear and stood her ground. If he wanted to hurt her, there would be precious little she could do to stop him. She stared at him defiantly. "Despite your doubts, my friends will be looking for me now," she said, hoping her voice sounded steady and confident.

He slowly looked her over as if calculating the odds of a particular action. "Then you'd better get on home before anything bad happens to you, don't you reckon?" Charley took hold of the tips of Becky's shirt collar and exerted pressure on the back of her neck. His breath stank of stale tobacco as he hissed a warning.

"And I won't be so nice another time, missy," he growled, fixing her for a moment longer with his boar's eyes before releasing her. He stood stolidly watching as she set off in the direction she had come, hastily stumbling with fear and fatigue, weighted down with her failure.

Sheila gasped at the disreputable figure darkening the kitchen door. "My God, Becky, where have you been? We were about ready to call the police." She surveyed Becky's sopping wet clothes, the muddy streaks on her face, and went directly to the refrigerator for a water tumbler full of orange juice. "Sit down and drink this," Sheila ordered, steering her friend into a nearby chair and standing over her until the glass was drained. "Now, where have you been?"

"On a fool's errand," Becky muttered blackly.

"I'll settle for that right now," Sheila shrugged. "You can fill in the blanks after you get out of the shower." She half-lifted Becky from the chair and marched her to the stairs. "Do you need help?"

"I can manage, I think," Becky mumbled, hauling her weary body up by force of will and the sturdy banister. "At least I know where to find the shower."

"Please place your newly scrubbed little fanny in this chair and tell me what in hell you've been doing all day," Sheila ordered reproachfully. "Gene and I were going crazy worrying about you."

"I'm sorry about that, but I left pretty early," Becky apologized, telling Sheila about Kevin's call and her subsequent search. "Like a dummy I went off on an empty stomach and didn't take anything with me. I guess my blood sugar was pretty low by the time I started back.''

"Pretty discouraged, too, I imagine," Sheila commiserated.

"Dammit, Sheila, it has to be there, but I combed every square inch of that creek bottom, and I can't find it." Becky slammed her fists against her legs in frustration. "I didn't find anything except some red-neck who scared the hell out of me."

Sheila set the chicken sandwich she'd prepared and a glass of milk in front of Becky. "This should help ease your stomach's condition, if not your mind. What red-neck?"

"Thanks, Sheila." She took a large bite of the sandwich. "Ummm, good. Some guy named Charley who works for United, if his shirt is genuine. I guess he's protecting whatever they're hiding. He's pretty convincing, too." She shivered involuntarily. "Listen, I'm sorry about worrying you and Dad. I didn't mean to be gone so long."

"Just leave a note or something next time, huh?" Sheila chided her. "You could have been hurt or something, and we wouldn't even know where to start looking."

Thinking back to Charley's menacing presence, Becky suddenly saw the reasonableness of Sheila's request. The sandwich and milk downed and a cup of coffee in her hand, Becky began to feel normal again. "All better now," she pronounced with a smile.

"I may be able to cure that," Sheila said wryly, pouring a cup of coffee and sitting opposite Becky. "I don't

mean to add to your woes, but we have a problem here
that I think needs your attention, too.''

"I have sort of left you holding the bag, haven't I?''
Becky flinched. "What is it?''

"Well, you may or may not have noticed, but business has been dead slow this week at best. This afternoon, I've had several calls to cancel big dinner parties
and business meetings that have been on the calendar
for weeks. I don't quite know what's going on,'' she
finished uneasily.

Becky's stomach began to contract. "What reasons
did they give you?''

"The usual excuses people give you when they don't
want to tell you the real reasons: sick kids, vacations,
relatives in town, changing to a later yet undecided
date. By the sound of it, I'd guess the word is out about
the fish kill and people are afraid to eat our trout.''

Becky sighed and shook her head ruefully. "I should
have listened to Dad and Kevin. I tried to make the
situation very clear for the City Council, but they may
have misinterpreted what I said...''

Sheila frowned, chewing her lower lip thoughtfully.
"That couldn't account for everybody, Becky. The cancellations aren't from people who frequent City Council meetings, and there was nothing in the paper about
what you said at the meeting. There has to be more to it
than that.''

Becky stared at Sheila, a knot of apprehension rising
toward her throat. "More? Like what, Sheila?''

"I hate to heap coals on your already battered head,
but I have a gut feeling—and nothing much more solid

than that—about it, Becky." Sheila sipped at her coffee before looking into her friend's worried eyes. "I think somebody out there is playing a very hard game of 'Rumor' with us."

"Are you saying someone is deliberately trying to ruin our business?" Becky asked incredulously.

"I'm saying I think it's an above-average good possibility," Sheila persisted, "that we need to investigate."

"But who would want to...."

"Maybe your phantom dumper is miffed at your interference," she suggested.

"But what would he have to gain by ruining my business, Sheila?" Becky's mind whirled in confusion at this possibility, too sinister to seem real.

"Think about it, Becky. You've been rattling a lot of cages. If you're getting as close as Kevin thinks you are, our villain may think a diversionary tactic is in order. Whoever he is, he's a businessman, and he knows you'll have to pull in your horns and concentrate on your livelihood. That leaves you less time to harass him, doesn't it?"

"Sheila, I can't believe anyone would do something like that to us. You know business is always a little slow in the summer."

"Honey, we're not talking the summer slows here. We're talking about no business at all if it keeps going this way," Sheila insisted. "We haven't had a week this bad since we opened three years ago." She paused to let Becky digest the information thoroughly. "At least check it out."

"How do I do that?"

"I don't know, unless you can find someone who

will tell us the truth about what they've heard. You might look over the cancelled reservations for a name you know well enough to talk to," Sheila offered.

Weary and bewildered, Becky got to her feet slowly. "I have to think about it, Sheila. Maybe I can figure out something. If you need me, I'll be upstairs."

After pulling the shades to darken her bedroom and reduce distraction, Becky lay across the bed, trying to sort through the jumble of thoughts racing through her mind. She didn't want to believe Sheila was right about a rumormonger, but what if she were? How on earth could they fight that sort of smear tactics? How could they publicly refute something privately spread?

Time was of the essence. Rainbow's End wouldn't last the summer if they couldn't stanch the flow of business they were losing. But how? If a rumor were at the bottom of it, Sheila was probably right about its source. Somebody was running scared because she and Kevin were getting too close. At least Kevin thought they were getting too close. After her day's failed expedition, Becky wasn't so sure.

She pounded the pillow. Why couldn't she find the damned pipe? How would they be able to prove anything without the discharge outlet? Her mind's eye rescanned the territory she had trekked over for some tiny, overlooked detail.

The door opened softly. "I hear you're having a bad day. May I come in?" Kevin stood framed in the door, holding something in his extended hand. As he approached the bed, Becky could see a single wild daisy winking its sunshiny eye at her.

"I'm glad to see both of you," Becky replied softly,

sitting up and opening her arms to him. "Come hug me a minute so I'll have strength enough to get to the kitchen for some milk. Ulcer prevention, you know," she explained wryly.

Kevin sat on the edge of the bed and held her for a long, quiet moment, stroking her hair gently and massaging her tense shoulders. "Want to share?"

"First the milk," she said, scooting out of bed, albeit reluctant to leave his arms. She raised the shades and squinted her eyes against the sudden flood of evening sunlight. "Come on into the kitchen in case I can't make it back in there," she joked skeptically. "Are you a cow juice fan, or would you prefer"—she examined the refrigerator's interior—"cranberry cocktail or iced rose hip tea. Those seem to be your choices."

"Cranberry is fine. I can use the vitamin C," he laughed as she filled each glass with the beverage of choice.

They sat at the little table near the window, overlooking most of the farm. Kevin listened quietly, sipping at the tangy ruby liquid as she recounted her unsuccessful expedition between sips of milk, carefully omitting her encounter with Charley and her conversation with Sheila. She finished with a small laugh. "So, I thought maybe if I went back to bed, I could get up and start the day all over. Maybe make it come out better."

Kevin studied her for a moment. "Are you sure that's all there is to the story? That doesn't sound like enough to send you to bed in the middle of the day." At her too vigorous denial, he dropped the line of questioning, at least for the moment. "Rough way to find out, but it sounds as if we're on the right track, doesn't it?" Kevin remarked too casually. "You covered the creek area thoroughly?"

"You will find scraps of my skin and fingernails under every rock and tree root along that whole stretch, I guarantee you. There just wasn't anything to be found, Kevin." Her eyes were huge and tormented.

"Then it has to be buried," he frowned. "We just have to get somebody from the state to look at the industries in that area. We have to identify the plant it comes from."

"How will that help find where it's coming into the creek?"

"If Pollution Control can find where it's leaving the plant, they can do a dye test."

"Do you know how to do a dye test?"

"There's nothing to it. All you do is dump some dye in the pipe at the plant and watch to see where it comes out into the creek. Why?"

"Is it a special dye of some kind?"

"Nothing I can't get hold of. What exactly do you have in mind, Becky?" he asked, one eyebrow rising suspiciously.

"A little nighttime vigilante work."

"Becky, you're talking about something illegal if we do it. It's all right for Pollution Control."

"Kevin, dumping is illegal, and we both know how much we can depend on Pollution Control, don't we?"

"No. Absolutely not." He crossed his arms adamantly. "Not a chance."

Becky laid her hand on his folded arms in supplication. "Kevin, not only is someone killing the trout, they're going to kill my business. Two can play at that game.'' She removed her hand and squared her shoulders defiantly. ''You can go with me, or you can get me the dye and I'll go alone.''

''Damn it, Becky, that's dirty pool,'' Kevin protested sturdily. He studied the stubborn set of her jaw and knew he was lost. ''When did you have in mind to go over the wall?''

She dazzled him with a smile and squeezed his arm. ''Thanks, Kevin. You won't be sorry; I promise.''

''I'm already sorry, and we haven't even decided when we're going,'' he responded wryly. ''I suppose we dress in black and smear our faces with charcoal or mud or some such. Isn't that how they do it on TV?''

''Something like that, I think. Are you free Friday night? Say, sometime after midnight?''

''I may not be free, but I'm very reasonable,'' he said, extending a hand toward her. She rose and came around the table to sit in his lap. ''Lucky I'm not a minor, because this would definitely be a contribution to my delinquency.''

''Not to worry. If we get caught, Mother and Sheila will mail us cakes and cookies.'' She snuggled against him.

''I don't believe I'm letting you talk me into doing this. What I ought to be doing is tying you to a chair to save us both from jail.''

''You talk too much sometimes,'' Becky said softly, stilling him with a kiss before moving back to her own chair. ''Did you think to ask Gordon about our recalcitrant councilman?''

''Of course, I did,'' he retorted indignantly. ''I take

orders very well, or I wouldn't be planning to break into a factory yard in the middle of the night."

"We're just going to look around, Kevin. At most, it's simple trespassing," she tried to reassure him. "Now, who is he, and what does he do?"

"Runs a paving company. He also, coincidentally I'm sure, heads up the city's industrial development committee. He's made a tidy little fortune off Oakdale's growth."

"That certainly explains his progrowth stance, doesn't it?" Becky said caustically.

"About Sheila's theory on your drop in business: Have you thought of anyone who might tell you if they've heard any rumors about the restaurant?"

"While you're eating, I'll look though the cancellations. I can't think of anyone right off hand. Mother knows a lot of business people through her church, but I'm afraid she'd have cardiac arrest if I told her what's happening, so I can't ask her."

"Have you or Sheila told Gene yet?"

Becky shook her head. "He has enough to think about with the trout farm. He doesn't need to think about this just yet." She fervently hoped they could find out and solve the problem without his ever having to think about it. "Sheila fed me when I got back, but I'll bet you're getting hungry, aren't you?"

"Can't deny it. Lunch today was yogurt and a peach." He grinned.

"Let's go. Yours may be the only meal Sheila gets to cook tonight." They walked down the stairs together to find fewer than a half dozen diners in the restaurant. Even for the early hour, the number was discouraging.

While they didn't discuss the situation further, the empty tables and lack of the usual bustle of business disturbed them at a deep level. The game was taking a deadly serious turn.

Douglas Price popped another antacid tablet in his mouth as he paced his office impatiently. Why was it taking so long for Charley to answer his summons? Things were not going according to plan, and Price was unhappy about it. He felt his control slipping, and he was determined to secure another hold.

He had spent the morning with the mayor and his friend on the City Council, listening again to their anxious account of the plea that Sherman woman made at the meeting. Price reinforced their fears about local industry resenting such meddling without justification. He pointed out, none too subtly, that United's one hundred jobs were nothing to dismiss lightly and reminded them who would be left holding the bag on United's plant facility if the company left town because of municipal harassment.

Price laughed to himself. If those fools had enough sense to realize it, they should be telling him what to do. The city was so eager for industry, they financed facilities and leased them back to the companies, gave them lower utility rates and whatever other inducements were required. It amused Price to have city officials at his beck and call, especially considering United hadn't paid a penny of taxes since it came.

A tap on the door interrupted his thoughts and his pacing. "Come," he snapped at the door.

Charley's square form appeared in the doorway. "Mr. Price, you wanted to see me?"

"Come in and close the door, Charley," Price instructed, moving behind his massive desk. "You know the little overtime job I assigned you for a couple of weekends? We're going to stop doing that for a while."

"Yes, sir. Trouble?"

"Nothing much, but some people had a few fish die on them, and they're trying to blame it on local industry. We just need to lay low until the fuss dies down."

"I heard about that, but I wasn't sure we had anything to do with it. According to Leo, that creek is a good ways across the hill from the trout farm."

"I didn't say we had anything to do with it, Charley," Price reminded him intensely. "What I said was they're looking for somebody to blame, and I want to be damned sure it isn't us." He reached into the drawer for another mint. "Tell security to check the area behind the plant with greater regularity after dark. I don't want any snoopers, even though I assume you've taken care of everything back there, haven't you?" The question bordered on menacing.

"Sure I have, Mr. Price," Charley replied indignantly. "Somebody would really have to know what they're looking for. It's set up to look like part of the normal equipment." He paused, looking at Price, his eyes narrow slits. "You do want security to...well, detain and question any intruders before they call the cops, don't you?"

"Especially if one of those intruders is that Sherman woman," Price instructed grimly.

"Wish I'd known that sooner." Charley grinned unpleasantly. "I sent some woman packing from the creek, and I'll bet it was her snoopin' around, now that I think of it."

"On the creek? Why didn't you tell me?"

"Wasn't sure it was her. Besides, she didn't find nothing but me. I scared her pretty good, I think, about coming back. She comes again, I'll see that she finds more than she's looking for." He leered at the prospect.

Price wasn't pleased to learn they'd identified the creek as the secondary source. He hoped his actions to endanger her business would get her off his back, but if worse came to worst an anonymous phone call would surely bring her back to the creek for Charley to see to.

"I know I can depend on you to take care of everything," Price said, dismissing him with a nervous wave of one hammy hand. "Just cover any tracks back to the company very carefully, and you'll be well paid for your loyalty, Charley." As he prepared to leave for the day, Douglas Price thought again about his retirement. He felt too old to play this kind of game, but he wanted his winters in Florida, and five more months of a clean record would get them for him.

Chapter Ten

Kevin arrived a little before the club closed on Friday night, wearing new blue jeans and a navy shirt. "Didn't have anything in spy black," he explained as Becky looked him over. "This is the best I could do."

"You do have on rubber-soled shoes?" she queried.

Kevin turned one booted foot up to show the sole. "As a matter of fact, I do. Why?"

"Don't cat burglers and spies always wear soft soles?" She grinned.

Kevin glared at her. "Go change your clothes and your attitude about this project. We're not going on a Sunday school picnic, you know."

She saluted smartly and ran up the stairs. Kevin slumped onto a step, leaned against the newel post, and kicked himself for the hundredth time. He knew they shouldn't be doing what they were getting ready to do. He also knew Becky was bent on going alone if he refused to accompany her. She didn't realize the dangers in dealing with the kind of people the dumpers appeared to be. He doubted they would stop at a little violence against someone in the obviously wrong place at the obviously wrong time.

If they were to have any chance of success at all, they would have to approach the plants from behind, and that meant up from the creek. Even after studying the city maps, Kevin wasn't sure just where the plants were in relation to the flags they'd left on the creek, but Becky assured him she knew the area well enough to navigate at night. He certainly hoped she wasn't exaggerating.

"Do you have the dye?" Becky asked as she returned, wearing black clothes and carrying her knapsack.

"Right here." He patted his shirt pocket. "I also have flashlights and a camera with high-speed film in the car."

"I have flashlights, too, and candy bars for quick energy," she said, smiling.

"Becky, one last time I'll say this: We shouldn't be doing this. Is there any way I can talk you out of it? Maybe seduce you into spending a quiet night with me?"

"But I will be spending the night with you, and we'll have to be quiet, won't we?" she shot back, then smiled blithely. "Are you ready to go?"

"As ready as I'll ever be," he groaned, getting up and starting for the door. "But I am going under protest. I'd like that put in the record, clerk."

She touched his arm. When he turned, her dark eyes were wide and serious. "Kevin, I promise you I wouldn't ask you to do this if there were any other way. I just don't see that we have a lot of choices right now."

"I know, honey, I know. If I had a better idea, you

can bet we wouldn't be setting off to trespass on somebody's property in the middle of the night. You do
know where we're going, I trust."

She shrugged. "More or less. The factories we're interested in are in the industrial park, and the two I want
to check are fairly close together. Both of them join the
creek, but on opposite sides of it. The buildings are
probably a half mile from the creek, but they're on
large tracts with nothing between them and the water. I
looked at a soils map today, so I have a pretty good idea
where they are in relation to the last flag we set."

"That's a long walk from here," Kevin offered,
"even in rubber-soled shoes."

"We'll drive up to a neighbor's pasture and walk
from there. It'll cut off a couple of miles. I borrowed
Dad's truck," she said, getting into the pickup parked
beside the house. She turned out of the driveway toward town, then cut off at a large farmhouse, driving
past the house, through a cattleguard, and into a pasture. "The creek is just down there," she said, pointing
past the headlights.

"What if the neighbor comes to see why somebody
is driving through his pasture in the middle of the
night?" Kevin asked uncomfortably.

"He won't. I talked to him earlier today. I explained
I have a biologist friend who studies some strange kind
of frog that only comes out after midnight, and that
he'd heard there were such frogs living on this creek."

Kevin groaned at her audacity. "Frogs. Ah yes, the
infamous midnight croaker. I remember him well.
Nothing like compounding a felony, I always say."

"Misdemeanor," Becky corrected him, "and I had

to tell him something. I thought it was pretty creative."
Becky knew she must sound flip to Kevin, but it was
her way of dealing with the jitters she had. She sounded
bold and she felt determined, but she'd never inten-
tionally broken a law in her life. She knew her parents
would die if they had any idea what she was up to tonight.

Parking the truck, they turned off the headlights and
fished the flashlights out of Becky's pack. They started
up the familiar creek, which seemed less familiar in
pieces the size of a flashlight circle. The overhanging
branches seemed consistently to take them by surprise,
and every hungry mosquito in the bottom must have
heard them coming. When at last the little orange flag
with the right number appeared in Kevin's flashlight
beam, Becky stopped to get her bearings before proceeding.

"The first one we try is about a half mile up on the
left. United is a little further past that on the right." As
they headed upstream, their progress slowed. The
water was deeper and faster, but the heavier brush on
the banks forced them into it more often. The slippery
rocks and swift current combined to sap their energy if
not their resolve. Both Becky and Kevin were breathing
heavily when she signaled they should be close enough
to leave the creek.

Making their way through the undergrowth, much
too noisily for Kevin's comfort, they reached a more
level area. They could see floodlights marking the
corners of the big plant a quarter mile away. When
Becky started for the lights, Kevin pulled her back.
"Hey, we don't just waltz up to the nearest security

guard asking for directions. We sit here a while to see what traffic is like before we cross the street."

While they waited, Kevin outlined the type of thing they needed to look for. "If they're dumping, they probably have some sort of sludge pond or tank where they hold the stuff until it gets too full. That's what we look for." Some thirty long minutes later, Kevin decided it was safe enough to proceed.

The moon was waning, so there was little in the way of natural light. Kevin was reluctant to use the flashlights any more than necessary, so the rough ground snagged their weary feet with painful frequency. They separated, each making large sweeps in the direction of the plant building, but the grounds were devoid of anything like a tank or pond, so Kevin signaled Becky back toward the brush. "I think you can mark that one off your list," he said, turning on his light and making his way upstream again.

Becky followed silently, disappointed at finding nothing, apprehensive at what must be ahead, hoping fervently Charley worked day shift only. At her signal, they once again left the creek bed to scramble up a deep embankment. Kevin was relieved to see that the woods thinned somewhat but continued nearly to the floodlighted area immediately around the building.

Again, they waited patiently and quietly for any sign of activity before beginning their search. At last they headed for the plant cautiously, unable to see all of the terrain for the scattered trees. As they emerged from the last of the heavy cover, Kevin pointed toward a hump in the ground that looked manmade. He doused the light and started toward it.

As they approached, the heavy, acrid smell of oil and solvents came to meet them, borne on the sultry air. "Smells like paydirt," Kevin whispered as they got closer. Holding his fingers over the flashlight like shutters, he shone the slivers of light toward the odor. They could see the embankment of a small pond, less than fifty yards from the back of the building, but well concealed in the trees and brush. They crept to the high side of the pond, where they could see its contents. It was two-thirds full of a black, oily liquid, only slightly thinner than sludge. Kevin quickly pulled a sample bottle from his pocket and scooped it full of the foul soup. He screwed the cap on securely, wrapped it in his bandanna and stuffed it into Becky's pack. As he closed the pack, he whispered into her ear. "There has to be a valve or pipe or something to take this stuff from here into the creek. Let's start looking at the low point of this pond."

Lights covered, they began a methodical search of the creek side of the pond embankment, trying to move quietly, but struggling through tall weeds and sprouts let grow, probably to hide the pond. Intent on their task, neither heard the man coming through the brush toward the pond until nearly too late. Before Becky knew the reason, Kevin had slammed her to the ground, her flashlight under her, one hand over her mouth, the other motioning her to freeze.

Becky was sure the pounding of her heart would lead the rustling footsteps directly to the spot where they lay trying to melt into the earth. Atop the embankment, the footsteps stopped momentarily and a strong flashlight beam began sweeping the surrounding area, closer and closer to their scanty cover. Her face buried in the dusty grass roots, Becky held her breath to a shallow token exchange and gripped Kevin's hand as the searching light reached the tall weeds above them and moved away at the same steady pace. They lay, afraid to move or even look up. The light had moved on, but they heard no movement from the light's owner. Becky felt perspiration dripping between her breasts and down her back. Fearing even the tiny sound of releasing Kevin's sweaty hand, Becky's fingers stiffened then grew numb.

After what she knew must be hours, the rustling footsteps receded toward the plant and finally passed out of the reach of their adrenaline-acute hearing. Only then did they breathe again, forcing down the sobbing gulps the lungs' deficit demanded.

Becky lay so rigid with fear that Kevin had to force her to her feet. "Come on," he whispered fiercely. "We probably don't have much time if he's walking a regular partol." They hastily resumed their search. Before she got ten feet away from their hiding place, Becky stumbled and fell heavily, flashlight rolling from her grasp, its suddenly unshielded eye exploding the darkness like a signal flare. Scarcely thinking, she dived to cover the glare with her body, pulling the lantern from under her cautiously, directing it toward whatever had tripped her. The dull gleam of brass contrasted with its surroundings of weedy growth.

Alerted by the sound of her fall, Kevin quickly made his way to her side. "What happened?" he whispered urgently.

She pointed to the big valve. "I tripped over it," she

explained as Kevin groped in the pack for sample bottles.

"Hold the light," he instructed as he scooped up samples of dirt and grass roots around the valve and wiped a sterile gauze pad around the threads and mouth of the valve with amazing speed. "That's good. Let's go. And move it: They may have seen your light."

They ran for the woods, not stopping until they reached the creek bank, collapsing there, panting for breath. "Kevin," Becky managed to say between gulps of air, "something's missing. That valve just opened on the ground. The stuff didn't just run down the hillside and into the creek, but I'm ninety-nine percent sure this is the place, aren't you?"

"We'll be a hundred percent sure as soon as I get chromatograms. These people aren't dumb, Becky. There's probably a pipe somewhere below that valve that goes to the creek. When they want to dump, they haul in a long section of pipe to connect the two points, dump the stuff and haul off the connecting section when they're through. It's a wonder we stumbled on the valve."

"We'll never find the pipe in the dark."

"Not very likely," Kevin concurred. "Besides, if this stuff checks out, we have the proof we need. Proof the state can't overlook." As he rummaged in the pack, his hand grasped the camera. "Damn, I forgot to take a picture. I'll be back in a minute."

Before she could protest, he was running back up toward the pond, alert as a hunted deer, but leaving Becky to worry about how much time he had before the guard returned. Like a hidden fawn, she sat wide-eyed but dead-still until a flash of light and a loud voice tore through the silent night.

"Is somebody there?" a man's voice shouted from the pond embankment. "Come on out. I'm armed." Becky could see his flashlight scanning the area, but heard nothing else for long moments. She fought the urge to race to Kevin, knowing he was safer alone, wherever he was. The guard crashed through the tall grass, searching and trying to convince the intruder to give up before reinforcements could be summoned. "Okay, it's your funeral," he shouted, heading back to the plant at a jog.

Within moments Becky saw Kevin's form looming in the shielded light from his lantern. "Let's get out of here," he whispered. "Head for the high ground and the fastest route back to the truck." Grabbing her hand, he set off at the quickest safe pace they could manage.

"I don't need a second invitation," Becky quavered. "I've never been this scared in my life," she admitted breathlessly, calculating the shortest cut to where the truck waited. "You look as cool as a cucumber, Kevin," she noted admiringly. "What happened out there?"

"Strictly show, my dear," he demurred as they hurried along. "I daresay this night has taken ten years off my life. I guess the guard decided he'd better double check the area, so he didn't go on to the plant when he left us. I'd just snapped a picture when I heard him coming back. He yelled, and I dived into some brush, using the noise he made to cover me. I guess he figured they don't pay him enough to take any chances alone, so when he went back for reinforcements, I lit out of there like a house afire. Becky, if he'd taken two more steps, he'd have been standing on my head. I wish you'd packed a bottle in your pack instead of candy bars. I could use a drink."

"Drinks plural," she corrected him with a shudder. "At least enough to stop my shaking."

Taking off their wet boots at the door, Becky and Kevin padded through the kitchen toward her stairs. "How's brandy?" Becky asked, turning toward the darkened club. "Isn't that what one drinks to calm the nerves?"

"Sounds good to me," Kevin answered wearily.

She returned with a bottle of cognac, and they trooped up the stairs, relieved to be safe and secure in familiar surroundings. Once in the apartment, Becky poured two glasses of the fiery liquid, which they both downed quickly with a minimum of sputtering. Handing Kevin the bottle, Becky headed for the bathroom. "I have to take a quick shower. I feel like I have creepy-crawlies all over me. I won't be a minute."

"I've got some dry clothes in my car. I'll run get them and follow suit, if you don't mind." As he returned to his car for the clothes, Kevin reviewed the expedition and knew they had gotten off lucky. Being caught wouldn't have meant a serious legal entanglement, but it would have been an embarrassment all around at the least, and if the guard had been armed as he said...he didn't want to think about that. He knew he could go home to take his shower, too, but he wasn't ready to leave Becky. The harrowing experience was too fresh for them to deal with separately.

When he returned to the apartment, Becky was just

coming out of the bathroom wearing a loose white shift like an extra long man's shirt. Kevin felt a rush of desire as the soft lamplight gilded her figure and her fresh scent wafted to him on the summer night. He contented himself with a quick kiss on his way to the shower.

Becky poured another glass of brandy and settled down on the sofa. Too bad tomorrow...correction, today...was Saturday, she thought. No calling Pollution Control until Monday. Her hands finally stopped trembling, her natural confidence began to creep back, and she pronounced it a good evening's work. She had what she needed to make it stick, if in fact the stuff they sampled tonight matched Kevin's chromatograms. Nobody would be able to push that under the rug. She could turn it all over to the authorities and focus her attention on other things of importance: her life, her business, Kevin.

As if in response to her thought, Kevin walked out of the bedroom wearing bathing trunks and a sleeveless T-shirt. Becky admired the muscular strength she saw in the exposed limbs, and she did so without dissembling. Her stare was so frank, Kevin picked up the hem of his shirt and looked down. "I did put on my pants, didn't I?"

"Oh, sorry for staring"—Becky smiled—"but you're so nice to stare at." A warmth began to spread through her, and it wasn't emanating from the brandy. Becky longed to have her problems behind her, to concentrate on Kevin without thinking about fish kills or chromatograms.

Kevin sat beside her on the sofa, pulling her against

him, where they sat sipping brandy and luxuriating in the feeling of their tired bodies in close contact. Hating himself for bringing it up, but knowing he had to ask, Kevin leaned his head against the sofa, stroking Becky's arm as if to ease the blow. "Becky, have you given any thought to what you're going to tell Pollution Control about those samples?"

She snuggled closer, murmuring sleepily, "I'll think about that tomorrow."

"I'm serious, Scarlett O'Hara," he persisted.

"What's to think about?" she replied, annoyed at his insistence on discussing business when she wanted to relax and cuddle. "I'll tell them where we got them, so they'll know where to go."

Clearly she wasn't computing what he was saying. "Becky, how are you going to explain getting them? Are you going to tell them we trespassed on private property in the middle of the night?"

Despite her resistance, Kevin's implication soaked through to Becky's brain. For the first time she realized she had created a dilemma for herself, and she sat up angrily. "Damned right I'll tell them I trespassed, if I have to. I had to do something if they were just going to sit on their hands, didn't I? Maybe I'll tell them an anonymous donor left them on my doorstep with a note."

"I just don't want you to start the conversation without having considered what to tell them," Kevin said calmly, "and I don't want you to be disappointed if they refuse the samples again."

She pulled away from him, a frown knitting her dark brows. "Why didn't you bring this up before we went?"

"Would it have made any difference to you? Would you have given up on going?"

"I might have," she said defensively, knowing as she said it how untrue it was.

"The moon might fall out of the sky tonight, too," Kevin said ironically.

"Well, at least your scientific curiosity is satisfied about the origin of the pollution," Becky retorted snidely. "Your scientific experiments are validated, so you can file them away...case closed."

"The case isn't closed until the polluter is brought to the bar of justice," Kevin replied patiently. "When the time comes, we'll be ready."

"Dammit"—Becky jumped up and paced across the braided rug—"I'm ready right now, Kevin. I'm tired of your jugsaw puzzle. I'm going to call Pollution Control first thing Monday morning, tell them what we have and, if I have to, how we got it. If they want to turn me in, let them, but I'm going to raise enough hell to make somebody listen to me and do something besides nod sympathetically."

Kevin sighed. "Becky, I told you from the beginning that this kind of thing requires a great deal of patience."

"The patience in this team is registered in your name," she snapped. "I'm in charge of anger. You tell me to be more patient. Well, I'm telling you I don't understand anybody who doesn't get mad about this." She stood before him, hands on hips, her eyes electric blue.

His face hardened. "I do get angry, Becky, but I learned a long time ago it's easier to get mad than to get things done. I use my anger differently. It fuels the hours of painstaking research you and your anger will need to bring this bastard to court and win." He stood, his compact body coiled like a steel spring. "I'm doing what I do best to help you, Becky, but don't expect me to do it your way. It's not my style to race around the countryside, raving about injustice and taking the law into my own hands. I don't get mad unless I can use it to get even."

Becky's hot rage subsided in the face of his icy resolve. "I'm sorry, Kevin. I just get so frustrated...."

"I understand that," he said, grasping her shoulders, "but you have to understand that there are many paths to the same place. Ours may be parallel, but they are not identical, and that's okay, Becky. It really is." He exhaled a long breath and visibly sagged. "I'll get the tests done by tomorrow afternoon, and I'll call you with the results. You'll know by then what you want to do with them." He took her face between his hands and kissed her gently. "Get some rest. I'll see you." She nodded wearily and walked to the door with him, mourning the turn the evening had taken but no longer blaming him.

Driving home in the predawn darkness, Kevin wished he weren't too tired to run the samples immediately. He felt sure they were the key so long sought. But there was the problem of what to do with them. The state couldn't approve of their collection methods, but they might be persuaded to go take a look on the word of a university doctoral student. Then again, they might not. As he turned in, he decided he was too tired to deal with it. One thing at a time was the way to proceed.

First the tests, then he would worry about what to do with the results... or worry about what Becky would do with the results, he thought wryly. That was probably closer to the mark.

Becky forced herself to dress and go downstairs by mid-afternoon, knowing she wasn't really needed to handle the trickle of business they would have. She knew Kevin was right about the problem with the samples, and she felt trapped on a not very merry-go-round, finding herself at the starting point again and again. Becky wasn't easily discouraged, but she felt lower than she had since the first kill.

Hoping the routine of getting ready for the dinner hour would help, Becky donned an apron and started preparing salad vegetables. The rhythmic rocking of the knife through the lettuce shreds seemed to restore her habit of thinking actively. If Kevin's tests showed what they expected, she would find a way to demand the state exercise its authority with United to get the evidence they needed. She would leave Kevin's name out of it if the trespassing came up, but she didn't really care if they knew of her clandestine activities. She felt she could make a pretty strong case for temporary insanity induced by bureaucratic bungling.

As she scooped the lettuce into the plastic container, the phone's shrill summons startled her. "Rainbow's End. May I help you?"

"Becky? Kevin. How are you?"

"Thoroughly demoralized, but on my feet. How are you, and how are the tests going?"

"I'm terrific, the tests are done, and you were absolutely right. It's United Industries, beyond question. The chromatograms match perfectly.'' He sounded proud and excited.

Caught up in his excitement, Becky made a snap decision. ''Bring everything you have out here to me, and I'll take care of it. I'm tired of being jacked around on the phone, so I'm taking everything to Little Rock on Monday, plop it on somebody's desk, and wait right there until I can come back with reinforcements.''

''I'll be out shortly.'' He signed off.

Until she heard her own words, Becky didn't know she had decided to go to the capital. She did know the place to start was at the top, with the people in the best position to expedite action. No more inspectors and receptionists, she would go to the director of the agency to make her case. Her spirits mended as she plotted her approach.

When Kevin arrived, he showed her the readouts. Even a nonscientific eye could see that the graphs were identical. He explained a few notes he'd made for her, after which she tucked everything into a briefcase retrieved from storage in an upstairs closet.

''I feel good about this, Kevin,'' she said brightly. ''This is what I should have done as soon as we knew what was going on. I may be a slow child, but I'm learning.'' She looked at him quizzically. ''Well, what do you think? You're so quiet.''

He chuckled. ''Not really, Becky. You haven't left many gaps in the air waves since I got here.'' Affectionately, he tugged at her earring. ''I think you're doing the right thing. Prepare for the worst, but hope for the best. . . . That's the only advice I can offer. Well, maybe one more thing: I'd try to talk to the same person who nailed the notice on Oakdale's door. Toughness counts."

"Thanks for everything you've done to get us to this point, Kevin. I wouldn't have had the patience, let alone the expertise to manage without you." She smiled sweetly.

"From each according to his or her talents, I always say. I'd be totally inept at what you're setting out to do," he shook his head and held up his hands in a gesture of surrender.

"Let's celebrate having got this far together," Becky proposed, eyes twinkling again at their usual voltage. "As soon as Sheila gets here, I won't really be needed tonight. Want to go do something wild and crazy together?"

"Wilder and crazier than what we did last night?" he asked in mock horror.

"More like what we didn't get around to last night," she whispered, combing her fingernails through his beard, "because of business."

A slow smile spread across Kevin's face. "Your place or mine?"

"Whichever is closer to the pizza place," Becky giggled. "I have a sudden burning desire for junk food."

"I wish I inspired the same reaction in you that a chili dog does," Kevin moped melodramatically.

"Who says you don't?" she responded playfully. "Where I come from, it doesn't take all evening to eat supper. Kevin, if I've told you once, I've told you a thousand times: Patience is a virtue you should develop."

She managed to duck through the door before his open hand connected with the portion of her anatomy for which he was unquestionably aiming.

Chapter Eleven

By five o'clock on Monday morning, Becky was on her way to the state capital, determined to see the Director of Pollution Control if it took a week of waiting on the doorstep. When the clock struck eight, she was at the reception desk. The secretary explained how busy the director was and asked if she could make an appointment for Becky.

"I've driven from the corner of the state this morning to see the director, and I'm prepared to wait here until I have done what I came to do," Becky insisted, glancing up at the tall, dark-skinned woman just entering the door with a briefcase. She wore her hair in a soft chignon and looked to be in her forties. Picking up part of the conversation as she passed, the woman smiled at the secretary, then at Becky.

"Can I be of some help here?" she inquired in a rich, interesting voice.

"I'd like to see the director with a problem I have," Becky explained politely. "I really can't talk with anyone else about it, but thanks for the offer."

"Let me introduce myself and reiterate my offer,"

the woman smiled. "I'm Janice Miller, and I am the director. Now can I be of some help?"

Taken aback but delighted to discover the woman Kevin had mentioned, Becky quickly introduced herself and assured Janice Miller that she certainly could be of some help. Following Janice into her office, Becky crossed her mental fingers, hoping she was right about a woman being more sympathetic to another woman. "Would you like some coffee?" Janice offered, picking up her cup off the desk.

"Yes, please," Becky responded. "Black."

While Janice went for the coffee, Becky pulled the sheaf of papers from her briefcase, wanting to be as organized as possible in her presentation.

Janice set a Styrofoam cup before Becky and moved on to her chair behind the desk. "Now, what's your problem, Becky?"

Becky outlined the whole story with brevity and precision: what had happened, whom she had talked with about it, and how she finally felt forced to trespass in order to get the necessary samples. She handed Kevin's chromatograms across the desk. "You'll see that they are a perfect match, straight across the board. They're labeled with the date and the site from which the sample came. One of your people was supposed to be up last week to check them, but no one ever showed."

Janice studied the chromatograms carefully and shook her head. "Becky, I would first like to apologize on behalf of the governor's administration, myself included. You should never have faced such a choice, but we've recently come to office, and our house is not yet completely in order. I do not mean to make excuses, but we do still have some deadwood to cull out.''

Becky suspected Mr. Gaines was in deep trouble at this moment. She rather hoped so.

''The inspector you spoke with was correct in stating that the agency does have policies regarding samples, but they are only policies, they are not law. Therefore, they are subject to interpretation and change as the situation warrants. Our people are well enough trained to investigate a situation and ascertain with fairly high probability the authenticity of the samples.'' She swept one long hand over the pile of papers. ''I hardly think you are likely to have manufactured all this for some petty, personal reason.'' She picked up the phone and asked the secretary to summon a biologist from the lab to her office. ''I'll have one of our lab men check these before you leave.''

Within minutes a young man with sandy hair and intelligent-looking eyes entered the office, his face questioning Janice. ''David, I want you to check this data for me and give me your best opinion of its validity,'' Janice told him, handing the stack of documents to him.

''Here are some more of Kevin's notes,'' Becky offered, passing the remainder of the readouts to David, who spread the papers along the end of Janice's desk and studied them quietly.

''Good work, Janice,'' he pronounced at last. ''The guy who did these is one of us. Definitely knows his stuff.''

Becky relaxed as Janice dismissed David with thanks and turned back with a smile. ''I know how tired you are of hearing that these things take time, but I have to say it again. However, I will call United Industries today and tell them a certified letter is on the way, notifying them of an investigation. In that letter I'll warn them to have all their records ready and not to tamper with the pond or anything around it prior to our visit. That should forestall problems for you until we can get there in person."

Becky frowned. "But isn't advance warning an invitation to get rid of incriminating evidence?"

A tolerant chuckle rippled over Janice. "Becky, you can't just make a pond and all the ground around it disappear like magic. These people may not be nice, but neither are they stupid. They know we wouldn't look kindly on fresh bulldozer work all over our evidence. I don't think you have to worry about that." She stood, graciously ending the impromptu interview. "It will probably be a week or two before we can get to you. We've had a couple of bad spills at train derailments, and they're keeping everyone hopping."

"I really appreciate your time, Janice," Becky said as she turned to go. "I finally feel like the good guys may win this one."

"We'll do our best," Janice promised. "By the way, if you do happen to find that pipe going into the creek, take a picture of it, will you?"

"You bet," Becky assented enthusiastically. "Thanks again."

Becky's steps scarcely grazed the carpet as she left the office. Oh, for wings instead of a compact car, she thought as she raced to the parking lot. She would have difficulty staying within the speed limit, urged by her desire to get home and tell everyone United's days... and its fines... were definitely numbered.

Douglas Price crumpled the transcript of Janice Miller's call in one angry fist and threw it against the wall. Damnation! he cursed silently, that Sherman busybody finally got someone to listen to her, and the state would be investigating United Industries. Home office would not be pleased by a lengthy investigation, he realized, reaching for another mint. As he chewed the chalky tablet, he realized he would simply have to bluff it through. After Charley removed the valve and covered the end of the pipe, Price could simply plead an accidental overflow of the pond, which he admitted was too big to hide so easily.

He sat like a coiled snake, tapping a pen on his desk at an accelerating rate. Damn that Sherman woman; she must have trespassed on plant grounds to get whatever she took to the state. In spite of his increased security, she had somehow managed to find enough to activate the normally sluggish bureaucracy, and she had to pay for that crime, Douglas Price decided. If he could come up with a plan to punish her and confuse the proceedings at the same time....

His eye fell on a trade paper in his basket with a regular column cautioning manufacturers about "The Dirty Dozen" environmental hazards that would bring the EPA down on a plant. A cold, reptilian version of a smile creased his face as the idea flickered to life. He picked up the phone and dialed an in-house number. "Charley, I have another little job for you."

After his conversation with Charley, Price dialed the mayor's office. "Mr. Mayor, we have a problem. The State Pollution Control Agency has notified me they are starting an investigation of our plant, based on evidence given them by Becky Sherman." His tone was injured innocence. "Well, you and I know it isn't true, but someone evidently believed her story. It's my understanding one of your city engineers helped her manufacture evidence against us, Mr. Mayor, and I must protest vigorously. He certainly doesn't seem to have the best interests of the city foremost in his mind, does he? He obviously has no idea how hard you work to keep area industry happy, to keep this community prosperous and its citizens employed." He listened to the mayor's self-serving excuses and his subsequent decision. "Well, of course, I wouldn't presume to tell you how to do your job, but I think that's probably the right thing to do, given the situation. I always appreciate your time and attention to my problems, Mr. Mayor. I'll be talking with you later."

The mayor was a stupid man, but a very useful one, Price thought as he cradled the receiver again. Trimble seldom understood the consequences of his actions until long after the fact, which was just the way Price wanted it.

Having stopped only for gasoline and a quick call home, Becky reached Rainbow's End in record time. She found Kevin, Sheila, and both her parents waiting anxiously for the news she refused to share until she got there in person. Affecting her best calm demeanor, she announced, "Ladies and gentlemen, I have just met the rarest of creatures: a government official who knows what to do and intends to do it. She is, of course, a woman." She smiled archly at Kevin.

"Who would ever think otherwise?" He rolled his eyes heavenward. "Did you see Janice Miller?" Becky nodded.

"Would you get on with the story?" Sheila demanded, handing her a large glass of iced tea and pointing to a chair.

Becky related every word of the interview she could remember, including Janice Miller's promise of action. "I really believe her. She's quite a woman; seems to be in firm control. She's living proof you get more done if you go right straight to the top."

"Well, I'm surprised at her lenient attitude about your trespassing," Frances said disapprovingly. "Rebecca, what ever possessed you to take Kevin traipsing around the countryside in the middle of the night? What if you'd been caught and arrested?"

Becky shot Kevin a malevolent look as the whole load of her mother's displeasure settled on her shoulders. Kevin grinned maliciously. "Well, Mother, you'd have had to come bail us out, I suppose."

Frances sniffed through pinched nostrils. "I'm not very happy about the way you and your father have been keeping everything from me, either. I didn't even know the restaurant was having problems until Emily called me."

"Emily who? What did she tell you?" Becky frowned.

"My friend Emily Wills from the church. She called to say she'd heard at bridge club that Rainbow's End was serving contaminated fish and losing all its business." Frances twisted her wedding band nervously. "I was so embarrassed to have to tell her I didn't know anything about it except that it couldn't be true."

"Did you ask her who told it?" Becky asked softly.

"Yes, but she couldn't remember. She overheard another table talking about it and didn't know who brought it up." Frances took a deep breath. "I want to remind both of you that I have invested thirty years of my life in this trout farm, and"—she looked at Becky directly—"thirty-four years in my daughter. Things that threaten the welfare of either are of interest to me, and I want to know about them."

Abashed, Becky attempted a lame explanation. "We just didn't want to upset you unnecessarily, Mother, but we were wrong to do it the way we did. I'm sorry, really."

Gene put his arm around his wife's shoulders. "Honey, I'm sorry, too, but just be glad it's all turning out so well. Would you really have wanted to know they were prowling around at United in the middle of the night? I'm relieved they didn't tell me until they were back with what they went for."

"Well, maybe not that part," Frances admitted, "but I still think...."

"This calls for a celebration," Sheila announced, going to retrieve a bottle of champagne from the club. "Becky, get some glasses," she called from the hall. When she returned, Sheila popped the cork and filled the waiting glasses. "A toast: to Becky for her perseverance... and to Kevin for his patience with Becky's brand of perseverance." Laughing, they all lifted their glasses, clinking them together happily. Sheila set her glass on the table. "Okay, enough of the celebrating. Back to work, Becky. You still have to figure out how to solve our problem of the missing customers."

Becky pointed a finger at Sheila as she finished her

champagne. "I thought about that on the way home. I'm going to call the newspaper and maybe the television station, asking them to do a story on us. We can refer them to experts to verify the safety of our fish, and we'll start advertising again when the stories break. That should do the trick, maybe not overnight, but I think people will respond when they know the truth."

"Good," Gene approved, setting his glass on the sink. "If nobody needs us, I'll walk Frances home then." He patted Becky's shoulder. "Good work, darlin'. See you a little later."

"G'night, Mother."

"Pretty proud of yourself, aren't you?" Sheila teased, squeezing Becky's shoulders as she passed. "Damn good reason, too, I might add. I sure hope this scheme works as well as the other one seems to have.... I get lonesome around here with nobody but a cooler full of trout, all dressed, and no place to go."

"Hang in there," Becky called after her, "good times are comin' again." She turned her attention to Kevin. "You should be pretty proud, too. You have the official state stamp of approval. They say you obviously know your stuff."

He threw back his head and laughed. "I can't tell you how relieved I am to hear that."

"Kevin, my faith in government really soared after talking with Janice. She seems determined to do a good job and apparently has the governor's backing to clean house if that's what it takes." She giggled. "I have a feeling our Mr. Gaines got his walking papers today, thanks to us."

"That may be the best thing to come out of today."

He grinned crookedly. "Makes room for somebody more serious about pollution than about retirement. Have you eaten yet?"

"I was holding out for an invitation to a seafood frenzy. Thought about it all the way home, as a matter of fact, and I think I could consume my weight in boiled shrimp. Interested?"

"You sound like a hungry shark"—he laughed, getting to his feet—"but consider yourself invited. I was thinking about another type of frenzy all this afternoon." He smiled slyly, his hand stroking the soft side of her neck. "Interested?"

"Consider yourself invited back here for dessert," she assented, rising into his arms. "Sounds like a thoroughly satisfactory way to celebrate a victory, doesn't it?" She kissed him, a sweet sample of the house specialty reserved only for him. "Hang tight while I shower and change. I always feel so grubby after a long drive, probably because my air-conditioning doesn't work very well when I go up hills. There are several between here and Little Rock, you know."

"Hurry," he said softly. "My mother always made me eat all my meal before I could have dessert, and I'd like to get started." He swatted her fanny as she passed by him and settled down to wait.

She was so ebullient, so sure the crisis had passed. Kevin wished he were as certain. It wouldn't really be over until the investigation was complete and the offender punished... and all the good guys in home free, he added grimly. He wanted it to be downhill from here, but he didn't trust United Industries to simply lie down and roll over. Whoever there had engineered not only the dumping but the damaging rumor about Rainbow's End wouldn't go down without a fight. Kevin snarled as he thought what he would do to that individual if it could be a fair fight instead of the insidious night-riding tactics that seemed to be his specialty.

Gene reappeared at the kitchen door. "Kevin, I want to ask you something, and I want a straight answer."

"I'll do my best, Gene."

"Is it really over like Becky thinks? Is it safe for me to put fish back in that pond now?" His blue-green eyes, so like Becky's but steely with suspicion, regarded Kevin steadily. "What do you really think about it all?"

"I don't really know what to think, Gene," Kevin admitted simply. "I kind of think it is. I hope it is. I'd like to think those people at United aren't stupid enough to pull anything else with the state on their case."

"I'm not the only one with doubts, I see," Gene surmised from Kevin's wishful wording. "I think I may put a few of the bigger trout back in that pond, but I don't think I'll put all of them back right away, Kevin. I don't think that would be a good idea, do you?"

"Don't much think I'd restock it completely right now," Kevin agreed. "Plenty of time for that later, I'd say." Like Gene, Kevin believed it was better to err on the conservative side. Miscalculations were easier remedied.

The newspaper and TV station were very cooperative, omitting the source of the pollution and the names of any responsible parties until the investigation could be completed. Page one of Wednesday's paper carried an otherwise comprehensive account of the whole affair. By Thursday afternoon people were beginning to call for reservations and to reschedule some of the dinner parties cancelled earlier. When Becky returned from the bank on Thursday, Sheila glowed with renewed enthusiasm.

"The phone has rung off the wall today," she bubbled. "Within a week we should be able to make mortgage payments again, Becky."

"I'm sure that will be a great relief to the bank," Becky commented wryly. "It will certainly ease my mind."

"Now that we're getting squared around here, you can concentrate on Kevin." Sheila smiled mischievously. "You know, he must be really bright to keep up with his schoolwork when he's with you almost all of the time he isn't working."

"Sheila, he's not with me all that much," Becky countered, a little uncomfortable with the line Sheila's conversation was taking.

"Just every chance he gets, huh?" Sheila grinned. "Don't misunderstand me...I approve wholeheartedly. I'm glad this trouble is nearly over so you two can talk about something besides fish and retribution. Have you talked about marriage yet?"

Becky was scandalized at her friend's assumptions. "Sheila, Kevin and I met less than a month ago. Let's not be hasty here."

"Becky, this is Sheila you're talking to, not your mother. It's obvious to even a casual observer how you feel about each other, and I'm far from a casual observer," she prodded shrewdly. Her voice lowered and her brown eyes narrowed. "Are you sleeping together?"

"Sheila! That doesn't come under the heading of your business," Becky gasped. She'd never discussed her love life with anyone, and she wasn't about to start now.

Undaunted, Sheila shrugged. "I know that. Well, are you?"

Deciding she'd had all this she could tolerate, Becky headed for the door. "That's for me to know and you to find out . . . if you can," she tossed over her retreating shoulder.

"I'll ask Kevin," Sheila threatened as Becky started up the stairs.

Becky laughed, shaking her head ruefully and thinking how few secrets she'd kept from Sheila over the years. Kevin was different, though. Very, very different to Becky.

Kevin reviewed the engineering reports a final time before heading to the conference room. The City Council voted to go with Kendall Engineering because they liked the split treatment idea, but at Gordon's request, Kevin went back through all the proposals in preparation for compiling the final plan that would be submitted to the state. The Waste Management Committee was meeting one last time to finalize that plan, trying to foresee any potential snags they had overlooked earlier. After the review Kevin was no more convinced than ever of the wisdom of the split treatment approach.

He was surprised to see the mayor in attendance.

Trimble sent Gordon in his stead to as many working meetings as possible. After calling the meeting to order, Gordon asked Kevin for his report.

Kevin sighed, knowing he was about to step on another land mine. "After reviewing the proposals, I believe there are going to be problems with split treatment, the largest of which is likely to be protests from landowners along Moore Creek. They are likely to object to a treatment plant in their neighborhood."

Several members voiced reactions. "They'll have to get used to the idea." "We don't have a better choice." "We all do things we don't like for the community's benefit."

"Secondly," Kevin proceeded as the comments died down, "I have serious doubts that EPA will approve these new rates for residential customers. They do have guidelines on residential rate structures, and I believe our proposal is an infraction of those guidelines. That leaves you with the necessity of also raising industrial rates."

"That's not an engineering judgment," the mayor snapped gruffly. "The City Council will decide who should pay for the necessary improvements." Although obviously addressing Kevin, the mayor studiously avoided eye contact.

Kevin shrugged. "All I'm saying is that I believe you need to be prepared for an EPA challenge to the proposed rate structure."

A businessman on the committee spoke quickly. "I'm sure the responsible people will take all this into account, but I think we need to give them the go-ahead to submit the plan as soon as possible. We're running out of time, so I think we should submit the plan as is and worry about any changes when the time comes.''

''I'm sure you've done a thorough job, Mr. Mc-Clain,'' the mayor said hastily, ''but your perspective is, of course, limited. You couldn't know, for example, that we are currently negotiating with two more industries who are considering Oakdale. We couldn't possibly hope to persuade them to locate here if we show them the rate structure you favor for industry. We may have enough difficulty keeping the industry we already have.'' He turned to the committee. ''Do I have a consensus to submit?'' At their nodded assent, the mayor adjourned the meeting quickly, leaving Gordon and Kevin sitting alone in the conference room.

Kevin looked at Gordon, a frown of puzzlement dominating his features. ''What the hell sort of exercise was that? Why was I making a report when their decision seems to have been made before I got here?''

Gordon stroked his tie thoughtfully, staring at the door where the mayor had so recently exited. ''I don't know what that was all about, Kevin, but I don't like it. When the mayor starts doing things on his own hook, it usually means trouble of some sort or pressure from somewhere he doesn't want me to know exists.'' He turned back to Kevin with a smile and shrug. ''Thanks for the work you did, even if they didn't want to hear it. Maybe when they hear it from EPA and Pollution Control, they'll remember who said it first.'' He unfolded his long legs and got to his feet. ''I think I'd better go see what Hizzoner is up to. See you.''

In response to the note on his desk, Kevin walked to

his boss's office and stuck his head around the door. "You wanted to see me?"

Kevin noticed how very uncomfortable this usually easygoing man looked just before he said, "Kevin, I don't know how to tell you this. Believe me, I fought it tooth and nail, but I'm outgunned, so...."

"Hostess, a bottle of champagne to be shared with my good friends, please," Kevin ordered as he arrived for dinner. "We have more to celebrate."

After a kiss of greeting, Becky looked at him quizzically. "We have? I must have missed something. What are we celebrating tonight?"

He smiled expansively. "Another new experience in my life, my dear. I got fired today."

Shock froze Becky's features. "Fired? Kevin, whatever for?" She couldn't believe she heard him right.

Kevin squeezed her and kissed her on the nose. "For fraternizing with the enemy, Mata Hari."

"How can they do that?" Becky sputtered as he walked her toward their table. "Who was responsible for it?"

"Came down from the top, according to my boss, who didn't like it but didn't have any say about it. Funny thing, I spent more time trying to keep him from feeling bad about it than I did feeling bad for myself. I never imagined I would react that way to being fired." He grinned widely. "Anyway, I think it's cause for celebration."

"Kevin, how can you celebrate such a patently unfair dismissal? I'd be calling a lawyer to sue the mayor's honorable pants off."

He took both her hands in his. "Believe me, Becky, they've done for me what I've wanted to do for myself ever since I went to work for them. I stand a good chance for a research assistantship in the fall, according to the head of my department. I'll be doing research in water quality to finance my education, not surveying streets and water lines. What more could I ask for?"

Unconvinced, Becky searched his face. "This isn't just a front to protect my feelings, is it?"

"Becky, I am a happy person tonight, a free person. Be happy with me, huh?" He grinned mischievously. "Of course, I was hoping the champagne would be on the house. I don't think I'm eligible for unemployment."

Becky laughed, in spite of her concern. "You can always bone fish or wash dishes, now that business is picking up again."

"If you think you're kidding, think again." Kevin wagged a finger at her. "But let's celebrate first and talk business later, okay?"

"Okay," she agreed. "I'll go see about some dinner. And I won't forget the champagne," she assured him as she rose.

Kevin's carefree expression transformed to a frown once Becky left. He was truthful with her about preferring the research position to his city job, but he hadn't shared his concern about the machinations behind his termination. Someone at United Industries had to be behind it, had to have convinced the mayor to do it. It wouldn't be difficult to twist that nitwit's arm, but what reason could they have other than pure spite? Kevin's work was done, United caught fair and sqaure. Firing him wouldn't prevent problems for United or the city; all it could do was punish him for his involvement. They had no way of knowing he wouldn't be devastated when they arranged the punishment.

What worried Kevin more than his own fate was the terrifying prospect of similar retribution aimed at Becky and her family. She was the public focus of the investigation, the prime mover in United's eyes, and that made her a primary target. This polluter was not the ordinary criminal dumper, getting by with whatever he could, paying his fines if he got caught. He seemed determined to exact revenge, to take down with him anyone in his reach.

Unconsciously Kevin clenched his fists at the thought of harm maliciously inflicted on Becky or her parents. As his love for this woman grew, his desire to shield her from hurt increased. Her new-penny brightness and impulsive delight in the world enlivened his too-predictable existence of recent years. Gene Sherman was one of the most decent men Kevin had ever met. The thought of some anonymous snake plotting in cold blood against people he didn't even know, people like Becky and Gene, filled Kevin with an unfocused but implacable fury, which he quickly shoved behind a smiling screen as Becky returned with dinner and the champagne.

Becky was a new woman since her conference with Janice Miller. Her natural buoyance was regenerating, her light, clever conversation sparkling again, and Kevin was delighted to see it. He decided he would keep his reservations to himself and revel in her aura of well-being. Maybe a little would rub off on an old cynic, he thought wryly as he toasted her health. "By the way, Becky, I have to tell you Sheila is trying to pump me about our relationship."

"You mean she asked if we were sleeping together?" Becky asked, her bluntness softened by her tolerant smile.

"Well, not quite like that," Kevin admitted, "but the bush took quite a beating along that line."

"She threatened to ask you when I wouldn't tell her," Becky giggled, "but I never thought she'd really do it. What did you tell her?"

"I drew myself up to my full height indignantly"—he duplicated his mock-innocent expression—"and told her I wasn't that kind of boy. Girls don't respect you if you're too easy or if you talk too much, I informed her and walked away quickly before I could break up and ruin it." He chortled and leaned toward Becky. "Do you think she believed me?"

"I think she's going to die of curiosity before she asks again," Becky laughed, happy to be in such a conspiracy with a man she loved, in a world getting back to normal, insofar as she could tell. She was still amazed that something so right was developing from so dreadful a beginning. Amazed, yes, and very content at this moment in her life, she thought, raising her glass toward Kevin with one hand, while she gave her lucky earring a little tug with the other.

Chapter Twelve

Friday morning Gene decided to move some of the larger trout from the fishout pond back into the pond where the kills occurred. Kevin had more free time now, so he and Becky offered to help with the move. They collected the last of the stragglers after lunch while Gene checked the fingerlings. The brassy sun beating down on their heads made the cool water feel refreshing on their feet, seeming to leach away the remnants of the last weeks' tension. Becky secretly relished working with Kevin, seeing more of him.

While they stretched out on the grass under a tree to rest, Gene's voice reached out to them. "Becky, come look at who's here," he called.

She raised up to see Gene strolling toward them in the company of a slim young man she couldn't identify at that distance. As he neared, she recognized him as an old classmate who worked summers at Rainbow Ribbon years before. "Leo," she greeted him, getting to her feet, "how are you? Gosh, I haven't seen you in years."

"Hi, Becky," Leo replied, dropping his head to

avoid eye contact, just as he had when he was sixteen. "I'm just fine. Yourself?"

"Great, Leo. This is Kevin, a friend of mine," she introduced Kevin as he got up. "Kevin, Leo and I went through school together, and he worked for us summers while we were in high school."

Kevin shook hands with the shy young man. "Nice to meet you, Leo."

"Leo, what are you doing these days?" Becky asked. "Have you married? Any kids? Where do you work?"

Gene laughed and held up a hand. "Becky, Leo didn't come here to fill you in on his recent history; he came to get some trout."

"Well, he certainly came to the right place," she said, grinning. "Do you have any dressed?"

"He wants them alive," Gene explained.

"Whatever are you going to do with live trout?" Becky queried Leo. "You're not going into competition with us, are you, Leo?" she teased.

"Oh no, ma'am . . . I mean, Becky," he replied seriously. "They're for my boss. His grandkids are visiting, and he wants some fish for them to catch in his backyard, or maybe just to look at. He didn't say for sure."

People often wanted to buy a few fish to put in a pond or pool at their homes, but they were seldom set up to handle the delicate trout, so the fish usually died shortly after leaving Rainbow Ribbon. Gene continued to sell fish for such purposes, but he had evolved a sort of warning label. "Leo, you know these fish have to have good, clean water that's cold enough and well oxygenated. What kind of place is your boss going to put them in?"

"I don't know for sure, Mr. Sherman. I never been there, but Charley, our foreman, says it's a real nice place. Got a little stream runs by it and everything. Anybody with that much money should be able to give them what they need." Leo shrugged. "I already told Charley they'd die if they wasn't in the right kind of water," he told Gene earnestly.

Becky flinched involuntarily at the sound of the foreman's name, the frightening afternoon flashing before her unbidden.

"Well, if you've already told them, it's okay, Leo." Gene slapped the young man's shoulder. "We just want to be sure everybody who buys live fish won't kill them with ignorance and blame it on us. How many do you want and what size?"

"He said get about thirty," Leo replied, starting toward his truck, relieved to get down to the business he came for. "I got a bunch of plastic garbage cans in the truck to take 'em in. I told Charley they'd have to go in the creek right away, though."

"Bring your truck down here, Leo, and we'll load you up. We'll have to give you some big ones and some little ones. A lot of the middle-sized trout were killed, and we need to save what's left for the restaurant," Becky smiled.

Leo shook his head sympathetically. "I heard about your fish dying. Downright shame, too. Ever find out what happened for sure?"

"We're still working on it," Becky assured him as she started for the nets.

They loaded the cans with fresh cold water and a half

dozen trout swimming in the confined space of each can. As Leo paid for the fish, Gene cautioned him again. "Get them where they're going as quick as you can, Leo. Good seeing you. Don't be a stranger." Leo waved as he drove away carefully. "That boy always was a good worker," Gene observed to Kevin. "I hope he's doing well for himself."

"Bless his heart, he's as shy as ever." Becky smiled. She turned to Kevin. "He doesn't come from a very good family. His daddy was a drunk, so he always sort of looked to Dad for advice and help. If he's running errands for the big boss, he must have come up in the world a ways from where he started. Good for Leo, by golly." She hoped, in passing, that Leo's foreman wasn't like the only other Charley she'd encountered lately. Someone like that wasn't good for anybody. But she was being silly: Leo wasn't wearing a United uniform, and there were a lot of Charleys in the world, she reminded herself. Still, the name stuck in her mind like a cockleburr in a dog's ear.

Douglas Price waited impatiently by the old cattle tank he'd ordered Charley to install near the creek on his farm. Charley should be back any minute with the fish, and the tank was ready for them. Charley was a good man, with not many scruples when it came to protecting the company's interests, and not prone to asking questions, however strange his boss's instructions seemed to him.

When Charley arrived with the plastic containers, Price indicated the tank. "We'll put them in here for now, Charley, and I'll put them in the creek when the grandkids get here tomorrow." If Charley thought it strange, Price knew he would keep it to himself.

"Leo gave me a long lecture... well, long for him," Charley laughed, "about how they had to be put in cold fresh water right away or they'd die."

Price flashed a serpentine smile. "Well, if they die, we'll just have to take them back where they came from, won't we, Charley?" His meaning was clear to his foreman.

"I reckon we could do that," Charley nodded. "Maybe I'll give them to that pretty little lady in person," he added with a nasty grin.

"Charley, I hope you realize the importance of discretion. None of this must ever be traceable to United Industries or to myself. The bonus in next week's envelope is for your caution in attending to this matter."

Charley tossed a careless salute and put the last can back in the truck. As he walked around to get in, he stumbled and looked down. "Where'd this old transformer come from? I haven't seen one like this for years."

"Beats me," Price said. "I suppose the electric company left it when they set new poles and lines through this area."

Charley kicked the broken cylinder. "Cheaper to leave them than to pay for disposing of them, I guess. Anything else you need, Mr. Price?"

"Do you think you could remove that valve below the sludge pond without leaving too many signs?"

Charley considered for an instant before nodding. "Yep, I think I can do that. I'll get on it right away. If you need me for anything else, you know where to find me."

Price dismissed him with a wave and turned to watch the rainbow trout glimmering in the late afternoon sun as they circled in their new quarters. They were pretty to watch, he had to admit. Maybe he really would get some for his grandkids some time.

Business at Rainbow's End was nearly back to normal on Friday and Saturday nights. Becky had sent some of her regular employees on their annual vacation when business fell off, and they wouldn't be back until Monday, so she recruited her parents and Kevin to help. It was a diversified but competent crew, with Kevin quickly picking up enough skills to work nearly anywhere he might be needed.

Saturday night the club did a lively business. The clock pointed in surrender to one o'clock before cleanup chores were completed. Becky, Sheila, and Kevin finished the required routines and flopped into chairs, frosty beers sitting before them.

"Hallelujah, tomorrow is Sunday," Sheila sighed. "I may sleep the clock around."

"You've earned every minute of it," Becky said with conviction. "I don't know how I would have made it through the past month without you, Sheila."

Sheila's head drooped toward Kevin. "Around here, you get lots of love and compliments, Kevin. It's cheaper than raises. Dumb old me, I can't seem to find anyplace I'd rather be, so I just keep soaking it up." She extended a foot to nudge Becky's leg affectionately.

Kevin chuckled. "Maybe she figures she'll never be

able to repay what she owes you in friendship, so why try?''

"Well, the first part is certainly accurate," Becky conceded, "if not the latter." She swallowed a long cooling drink of her beer. "Listen, I hate to break up an act that obviously works so well, but I've got to get up those stairs before I fall asleep in this chair."

Sheila finished her beer and stood up. "Think if you had to drive five miles before you could collapse. I'll let myself out and lock the front door." She winked. "Kevin can use the back door when he leaves."

Kevin feigned injury. "Oh, no. You mean I have to leave tonight, Becky?"

"I'm surprised I have any semblance of sanity to my name, considering my close association with you two," Becky grumped as she passed between them, headed for the stairs.

Kevin caught her in his arms. "At least send me away with a kiss to remember." His lips descended slowly, calling to hers. Her arms slid around his neck, and her tired body molded its curves to his shape like a garment. Through their sensual haze a distant voice bid them goodnight, but they never really noticed when Sheila left them to each other and slipped out into the night with a smug smile on her face.

Hours later, Becky roused herself long enough to wonder what on earth Major was barking at so persistently. Gene's old dog seldom barked at night, preferring undisturbed slumber on his rug, but he was raising the devil about something. Probably his favorite possum, she decided sleepily, looking for an excuse to stay right where she was happily ensconced. She dozed off again when Major's barking finally stopped without her intervention.

Charley wished the damned dog would shut up. It barked loud enough to wake the dead, and Charley knew the Shermans lived on the farm. He waited silently beside the dark hulk of the hatchery, hoping the dog would give up and go back to bed. When no light flared in response to the dog's alarm, Charley decided the coast was clear enough to proceed.

Quietly and quickly he dumped the trash bag of dead fish into the ponds. Price called to say the fish were dead and he wanted them taken back to the farm, but he wasn't specific about where he wanted them dumped. Charley scattered a few in the farthest ponds from the road, but the bulk he hurriedly emptied into the nearest pond, wanting to be gone as soon as possible.

Charley had a feeling there was a lot more to this than returning unsatisfactory merchandise, but it wasn't any of his business, he was well paid for the errand, and he wasn't going to lose any sleep over it. He learned a long time ago that the way to get ahead was to listen close, ask no questions, and do what the boss told him to do. This was not one of the best assignments Price had ever given him . . . not nearly as much fun as his idea for dealing with Becky Sherman would have been . . . but he couldn't be choosy, he thought, melting into the shadows toward where he left his car. He might still have a chance to deal with her if Price's plan didn't work well enough.

Unable to open his eyes, Kevin dragged the screaming telephone off the nighttable and laid the receiver on the pillow against his ear. "McClain," he muttered groggily.

"Kevin"—Becky's anxious voice roused him—"I know you've probably just got to sleep, but it's happened again. Dad just called me, and I told him not to touch anything until you got here."

Kevin shook his sleep-muddled head. "Give me ten minutes," he mumbled, threw the receiver into its cradle, and reached for the clothes so recently dropped on the chair beside the bed.

After she called Kevin, Becky threw on her clothes and scrambled down the back path to the ponds where Gene stood staring at over a dozen white bellies floating on the surface of the pond nearest the road. She could see flashes of white on other ponds as well. Her father's shoulders were rounded, and he looked older than usual. "I found them when I came down to feed," he said numbly. "I thought it was all over, Beck. At least it's not so many this time."

Becky stood beside him, her arm slipped through his in what small comfort she could offer. "Dammit, it is supposed to be over." They stood without moving until Kevin's car careened to a stop near them. Kevin ran toward them, lab pack slung over his arm. He set down the pack, gave Becky a quick squeeze, and surveyed the scene. "What happened, Kevin?" Becky asked quietly. "I thought it was all over. What could have happened?"

"I don't know, sweetheart, but I'll find out." He began pulling things out of the pack. "You two go on to the house, and I'll clean up here."

"I'll help," Becky said quickly. "Dad, why don't you

see if Mother could start some breakfast? We'll be up in a few minutes.''

Gene nodded and started toward his house. Before going far, he turned back to Kevin. ''Kevin, there's something different about this one. I can't put my finger on it yet, but something's not right. Keep that in mind.'' He walked on, carrying his cap in one hand and running his fingers through his gray hair as if he could rake out the significant difference he couldn't pinpoint.

Kevin and Becky started dipping dead fish out of the ponds and into buckets. Kevin's voice showed the stress he felt at this unexpected incident. ''Becky, get some paper out of my pack and note how many fish were in which ponds, along with their approximate size, will you?''

Clipboard in hand, Becky took notes as Kevin worked and dictated. When they finished, they loaded the buckets onto a cart. ''I'll take some of these to the lab for testing, and we'll put the rest in the cooler. We'll send some to the state lab in the morning.'' While Becky wheeled the grisly burden into the cooler, Kevin neatly repacked his equipment and the notes Becky turned over to him. ''Okay, let's go on up to Gene's,'' he said, frowning. As they walked past the ponds, he continued to stare at the fish remaining in the ponds, going about their normal activity.

Becky stopped and stood to watch for a moment. ''Dad's right, Kevin. It wasn't like this last time, was it? And the fish I put in the cooler didn't look the same. The color was wrong. Will your tests show how long they've been dead? I think that may be important.'' A pertinent thought tried to surface in her mind

but couldn't slip past the debris of her anxiety to retrieve it.

Before Kevin could answer, Major joined them,
frisking for attention. "Crazy old dog," Becky scolded
as she thumped him on the side, "up all night howling
at the moon or something equally sinister, no doubt.
Act your age." As they reached Gene's back door, Major settled on his rug to catch up on his sleep.

Breakfast was deliciously prepared, but somberly
consumed. Frances fussed over Gene, trying to ease
some of the burden rounding his shoulders, while
Becky racked her brain for anything Kevin might be
able to use. When the coffeepot was drained, Kevin
stood. "I'll go get started on the fish. Something isn't
right about this kill, and I want to know what it is.
Thanks for breakfast, Frances. It was delicious, as
usual."

Becky walked out with him. "Will you be back today?"

He hugged her tightly. "I'll be back as soon as I can,
honey. Try to get some rest." He set off down the hill
to collect the fish, his pack, his car and his composure.
He could feel the awesome white anger collecting in
him as a glacier accumulates layers of ice. This was to
be the Shermans' punishment, was it?

When he reached the university lab, he quickly
opened a fish and removed the gills. He passed over
the usual tests, operating on hunch and his suspicions.
The computer in his scientific mind scanned the details
of this morning's scene for discrepancies. Suddenly, he
knew what was wrong about today's kill: Most of the
dead fish were in the pond next to the road, not in

the pond where the fault opened. Only a few white bellies floated in the pond where the other kills had been confined. These fish must have died from some other cause.

Kevin examined another fish carefully. He concurred with Becky's assertion that the fish looked to have been dead for at least twenty-four hours. The scales and skin looked different from the fish he'd seen killed during that long night at Rainbow Ribbon. He prepared slides of the gills and the fatty tissue, not looking for suffocation this time, but for some toxic substance like heavy metals or one of the deadly chemical or organic compounds.

Next, he carefully dissected the fat from several trout, mixed it with solvent and prepared the solution for the chromatograph. After what seemed to Kevin an unbearably long interval, he had a good chromatogram whose pattern he could begin comparing to the EPA standards until he found a match. Kevin stared in horror at the legend beneath the matching chromatogram: "PCBs—polychlorinated biphenyls—a toxic compound found in transformer and capacitor oil." He remembered newspaper stories about the hundreds of dairy cattle killed and their owners sickened by PCBs somewhere up north. But how could PCBs get into the trout ponds? How? He rubbed his temples, attempting to retrieve anything he'd ever read about the substance, but the major thing he remembered clearly was its toxicity: two parts per billion would kill fish. That meant a drop of the stuff in one of the ponds would be enough to kill every fish in it.

He stood and started to pace. But all the fish weren't

killed in any of the ponds; there were a few dead ones
in several ponds. It just didn't fit. He sat on a lab stool
and stroked his beard absently, trying to fit the pieces
together. Suddenly his hand froze in a downward
stroke as the thought hit him. The fish were killed
somewhere else and dumped into the ponds. That had
to be what happened. It all fit together that way, but
would anyone else buy his theory? He sat for a moment not wanting to believe that anyone would do
something like that. Then the full import of the action
dawned on him. The trouble was just beginning, and
Becky had to be prepared for it. Carefully storing his
samples and gathering up the data, Kevin started for
the farm.

He found Becky in her apartment when he arrived.
Her smile of greeting sobered instantly at the look on
his face. "I'll make some coffee while you tell me what
you found."

"Maybe you'd better just sit down and hear me
out," Kevin suggested. "Becky, I found a substance
called PCBs in the fish." He explained as simply as possible what he knew about the compounds. "They are
very carefully regulated, and the Feds presumably
know where all of them are at any given time. The only
supplies not currently accounted for are some still rattling around in old transformers and capacitors." He
drew a deep breath and plunged to the heart of the matter. "Becky, I think those trout were killed somewhere
else by exposure to PCBs and dumped in your ponds
after they were dead."

She stared at him incredulously. "Dad and I talked
about it after you left, and we agreed something was very

strange about those fish, but we had no idea it would be anything this strange. Why would anyone want to kill trout with PCBs and dump them out here, Kevin?''

"I don't know for sure, sweetheart, but I'd guess as a red herring to confuse the investigation. These compounds are so toxic, they lay ordinary petro-pollution in the shade. I'd guess somebody at United hopes the uproar over this will distract the authorities from any other investigations."

Becky shook her head. "Then we won't tell anybody, so there won't be any uproar."

"We can't do that, Becky," Kevin said gently. "We have to report this tomorrow. We'll send some of those fish to the state lab on the first plane out in the morning, but I'm ninety percent sure they'll find what I found."

A fearful look crossed Becky's face. "Kevin, are you sure they were dumped here? The ponds couldn't be poisoned, could they?"

"If PCBs had really found a way into your ponds, there wouldn't be a fish left alive on this place, Becky," he reassured her firmly. "It has to be a setup. It's the only explanation fitting all the facts."

Becky stood. "Now I'll make that coffee, while we figure out who did it, why, and how we prove it," she said with grim determination, walking toward the kitchen. "Will the state buy your theory?"

"I'd say our best bet is Janice Miller, wouldn't you? She sounds like a pretty reasonable person."

"I'll call her first thing in the morning, tell her what happened, and what we think about it. What happens then?" She returned with two mugs of instant coffee.

"I'm not really sure," Kevin admitted. "I've never been involved with PCBs, but I assume they would have to report anything that dangerous to someone else, probably EPA. I don't really know what the procedure is."

Becky set her coffee down and looked at Kevin with a sad smile. "And just when you thought it was safe to go back in the water...."

Becky was on the phone to Janice Miller early the next morning while Kevin took the fish to the airport for the first flight. Becky explained what had happened, what Kevin's tests showed, and what they suspected about the planted fish. When she finished, silence flowed into the gap in her narrative. "Janice, are you still there?"

"Yes, Becky, I'm here, trying to believe nobody would go to such lengths to cover their tracks, but knowing you're probably right." She sounded weary and disappointed. "I'll send someone out to the airport for the fish, and we'll run tests this morning. I'm inclined to think your biologist friend is right about the fish being dumped in your ponds, but I'll still have to call in EPA and the health department. With anything as toxic as PCBs, we can't take any chances." She paused, then spoke in a softer tone. "Becky, it's going to be difficult for you until we can get this sorted out. They'll probably close the restaurant, or at least the trout farm."

"Close them?" Becky echoed numbly.

"Probably, at least until they're satisfied the source of the toxin isn't still there."

"For how long? Is there anything I can do to expedite?"

"The only thing you can do is wait. We'll take care of everything else. I'll have a man up there on the next plane."

After Becky hung up, she thanked her guardian angel for having met Janice Miller when she did. She might have to wait, but she suspected the wait would be shorter for Janice's efforts. Becky certainly hoped so, because she could be facing ruin if the whole thing weren't settled out rapidly. Becky had been able to explain away the two other fish kills, but if word got out their trout died from something like PCBs, that would be the end of the Shermans' trout enterprises.

Kevin promised to come to the farm after his early class, knowing the traffic would begin to pick up as soon as Becky called the state. He arrived at the same time as the man from Pollution Control, who immediately set about collecting samples of water and live fish to take to the state lab.

Around noon, the state inspector asked to use a phone. When he finished, he turned to say Kevin's tests were confirmed. "It's definitely PCBs. Someone from EPA will be here tomorrow. I'm heading back to the lab with these samples, and I'll let you know what I find out."

After he left, Becky questioned Kevin. "Why did he take the live fish?"

"To check for accumulation in the fatty tissues. If he doesn't find anything, it will support our theory that the dead ones were dumped here," he explained.

Becky slumped into a chair. "So what do we do

now?'' She chuckled at her own question. ''I wonder how many times I've asked that question in the past month?''

''And I wonder how many times you've been answered with 'just wait.''' He smiled wryly, rubbing the tension from her neck. ''This time we wait for them to find the source and hope they do it in one hell of a hurry.''

When Becky started down the next morning to help Gene feed the fish, the parking lot by the ponds looked like a convention had come to town. She could see several men clustered around her father, and she knew the parade had started. Before going down the hill, Becky called to alert Kevin, who said he'd be right out to see if he could help.

Becky stepped boldly into the group of men. ''Hi, I'm Becky Sherman. Are we holding a news conference here or something?''

Gene introduced two inspectors from the health department, and the EPA inspector introduced himself. The fourth man Becky recognized as the reporter she'd talked with about the previous fish kills. She smiled at the three officials and turned to the reporter curiously. ''What are you doing here? Surely the state didn't notify the newspapers, too.''

''I got a call this morning there might be a story out here again, so I came along to check it out,'' the man explained with a shrug.

''A call from whom?'' Becky queried, walking him a little distance away from the other men.

''Didn't give a name. Just said there had been a fish kill that might interest me.''

Becky flashed through the possible headlines. "Listen, will you do me a favor? Will you hold off just until we can talk to the rest of these people and find out what's going on here? I promise I'll talk to you when we're through."

"No problem," he replied. "I'll just take a walk. I need the exercise anyway."

"Thanks." Becky flashed a grateful smile and hurried back to the group around Gene. "Before you get started here, I have one pertinent piece of information for you," she offered, wishing she'd had time to tell her dad about Kevin's red-herring theory before announcing it publicly.

One of the men from the health department listened skeptically. "I suppose it's possible, but it seems pretty unlikely to me."

The young man from EPA was more cautious. "We're not discounting that or any other possibility, but we have to make a completely thorough investigation, starting right here. The compounds in question are so deadly, we have to be absolutely sure they're not in this ground or water. Once that's certain, we'll search farther afield."

"But how long will that take?" Becky asked.

"A couple of days at most," he shrugged.

"Meanwhile," the health inspector said, "we'll have to quarantine the trout farm."

"What about the restaurant?" Becky inquired.

"No problem, so long as you don't serve trout from this farm until we've okayed it," he assured her.

"Would you come to a trout restaurant for hamburgers?" she retorted sarcastically.

The young man was sympathetic, but firm. "We're sorry, but we can't take any chances with this. Can you buy trout from another source temporarily?"

"I'm continually surprised by the things I can do when I have to," she commented unhappily. "What about him?" She pointed out the journalist walking around the ponds. "Does he have to know?"

"I'm afraid so," a health inspector replied. "At least, we can't refuse information about an investigation without risking a Freedom of Information suit."

Becky considered the irony of that two-edged weapon, the Freedom of Information Act. "In that case, why don't you close the restaurant, too, while you're in the neighborhood?" She smiled bitterly at the inspectors.

Gene laid a hand on his daughter's shoulder. "Becky, these men are just doing their jobs. All we can do is cooperate with them and hope they find what they need in a hurry." He looked up at the sound of Kevin's car driving in. "The young man coming here is the biologist we mentioned. He can tell you more than I can."

After introductions, Kevin quickly summarized his findings from the first fish kill, how they differed from the current situation, and the results of comparisons made with materials from United Industries. "We believe this incident was staged in retaliation for our instigating an investigation against United."

"Sounds like you might have a pretty good case," the EPA inspector commented. "We're coordinating with the state, of course, and if they're willing to accept your tests, it's okay with us. Our concern right now though is not a fish kill caused by petroleum products, but PCBs floating around in this area. You know they have to take priority. We'll check with United to see if they have any PCBs registered in inventory, but it's unlikely, and if they don't, it'll be hard to prove your connection.''

Kevin nodded, hearing nothing unexpected.

"Gene, we won't give anything to the press that we don't know for a fact," the health inspector assured him, "but we will have to talk to him."

"If you'll excuse us, the sooner we start, the sooner we finish," the young man said, returning to his car for the necessary equipment.

Obviously dismissed, Kevin and Becky walked to the house with Gene. Disheartened, Becky said, "I guess we might as well close Rainbow's End if we can't use the trout."

"Don't go off the deep end," Gene cautioned her. "I'll go up to Al's today and get enough to last us a couple of days." Al was a friend of Gene's who raised trout twenty miles north of Oakdale, and Becky knew Al would give Gene whatever they needed. "Don't worry, honey, we'll get by."

"Get by?" Kevin echoed. "We'll do better than that. Come on, Becky. Here you have three of the finest minds of our time at your disposal. Don't waste them on self-pity," he prodded. "While Gene goes for the fish, I have a little idea you and I can bat around, if you're up to it," he needled.

"I'll make you think 'up to it,'" she threatened, eyes flashing deep blue sparks at him. "Dad, you go to Al's while I teach this uppity hired hand a thing or two about what we mean by 'getting by.'"

Gene laughed. "Boy, you're in for it now. Sure you don't want to go north with me?"

"I'm nearly as tough as she is," he said, grinning. "I can take anything she can dish out, Gene, but thanks for the offer."

When Gene's truck had turned down the driveway, Kevin sobered. "Becky, I think I know where those fish came from, and we need to talk about it."

Chapter Thirteen

For an instant Becky thought Kevin was still joking. When he turned to face her, she knew the kidding was over. "Kevin, what are you talking about?"

"I'm talking about tracing those fish back to the source of the PCBs," he said, grabbing her hand and walking rapidly toward the restaurant. "Make me some coffee, and let's talk it over together."

Mugs in hand, they settled onto Becky's sofa. Kevin blew across the steaming surface of his coffee while he organized his approach. "Becky, do you remember the man who bought the trout last week? The one you went to school with who used to work here?"

"Leo? Of course I remember."

"Okay, do you remember how many trout he bought?"

"Around thirty, wasn't it?" Becky couldn't see where the line of questioning was going.

"Becky, we found twenty-seven dead trout in the ponds on Sunday morning," he said flatly. "See any possible connection?"

She stared at him in disbelief. "No, I don't. Leo

would never do anything to hurt Dad, Kevin." That possibility tried to make its way into her awareness during the night, but she refused it entry.

"I'm not saying Leo did anything but buy trout for his boss, just as he said he was doing." Kevin sipped at his coffee, giving her time to absorb the idea. "I doubt that he had any notion of what his boss really wanted them for."

"Kevin, Leo is a decent person who would never be involved in the sort of thing that has happened to us," Becky protested.

"If he knew what he was doing," Kevin modified her assertion. "It wouldn't hurt to ask him about it."

"Leo would be mortified if we accused him of a thing like that."

"Not accuse, ask."

"Even to ask would be to imply his involvement, Kevin. You don't understand what kind of life Leo's had, and if he's getting along as well as he seems to be, I don't want to throw a monkey wrench in that." Becky folded her arms and turned away from Kevin.

"We could at least find out where he works," Kevin suggested softly. "What would be the harm in that?"

She turned, grasping in her distress for any other explanation. "Whoever did this surely wouldn't be stupid enough to buy the fish from us, then dump them back on us, would they? They would buy them someplace else, if they have any sense at all. I'll ask Dad to check with the other area trout farms to see if anyone bought live fish from them during the past few days."

"That might be precisely the reasoning they expect you to use, Becky. Buying the fish here might be a very smart move on their part. Please think about talking to Leo if the inspectors don't find anything to go on, okay?''

She nodded wordlessly, hoping it wouldn't come to that.

When Becky and Kevin drove into the restaurant's parking lot at six, Sheila's was the only other car in evidence. Frowning, Becky walked into the deserted dining room. ''Sheila?'' she called out.

Sheila came from the club, a glass of Irish cream liqueur in one hand, the evening newspaper in the other. Without a word, she handed it to Becky and went back for two more glasses.

LOCAL TROUT FARM UNDER INVESTIGATION: PCBs FOUND IN FISH. The article was dead center of the front page. Becky closed her eyes and handed the paper to Kevin.

'' 'State and Federal investigators arrived at the Rainbow Ribbon Trout Farm this morning after fish found dead Sunday were discovered to be contaminated by deadly PCBs,' '' he read aloud. He scanned the rest of the article rapidly and threw the paper aside. ''Nothing here we don't already know.''

''Does it mention Rainbow's End will be closed tonight?'' Becky whispered, too stunned even to cry.

Sheila returned with two more liqueurs, handing one to each of her friends. ''Becky, honey, they'll get it cleared up. We'll take tonight off, but we're not folding our tents just yet.''

''Have Mother and Dad seen it?'' Becky asked, afraid to hear the answer.

Sheila nodded, unwilling to relate the painful scene

with Becky's parents. "They were up earlier. They're pretty solid folks, and they'll be okay, Becky. Worry about yourself."

"Go on home, Sheila. I'll be okay, too. Go watch a movie, for a change." Becky smiled wanly.

"I'll stay with her," Kevin offered, standing behind Becky's chair, gently massaging her shoulders. "Is there anything we need to do before we go upstairs?"

"No, the paper came out before I got very far in tonight's preparations. After I read the article, I went for a drink and let the rest of it slide," Sheila replied. "Just turn out the lights."

"The party's over," Becky sang a soft finish to Sheila's exit line, ending with a long, sad sigh. "Kevin, I can't decide whether to cry, swear, throw crockery, or just curl up in a fetal position. I've never worked so hard in my life to end up with so little to show for it." She sat limply, her hands clasped in her lap as if to hold herself together.

"Come on, let's go upstairs," Kevin urged gently, pulling Becky to her feet. "At least we can be miserable in greater comfort there."

They trudged up the stairs heavily. "Are you hungry?" Kevin asked as Becky collapsed on the sofa. "Unfortunately I tend to eat under stress, so I'm starving."

"Not really," she said without animation, "but help yourself to anything you can find."

While Kevin rummaged through the refrigerator and cabinets, Becky kicked off her shoes and stretched out on the sofa. For the first time since the whole thing started, Becky felt really hopeless. Even if the inspectors found the source of the contamination, her business was ruined. The article setting the record straight would be on the back page with capsules of world trivia. The people habituated to reading the back page would still wonder what the truth of the matter had been and decide it was safer to eat somewhere else than to take a chance.

"Would you help me eat an omelet?" Kevin asked from the kitchen. "I've found enough ingredients for a good one, I think."

"Sure, why not?" she replied with a notable lack of enthusiasm. Four years work, all of her savings, her credit rating, she could visualize all of them whirling in a vortex down a giant drainhole. But she was young enough to start over, to do something else with her life. What about her parents? The farm was paid for, but they needed the trout to make a comfortable living. They were nearing retirement age, but farmers could seldom afford to retire.

"Come and get it," Kevin sang out. "Delicious hot omelet, whole-wheat toast, and milk...but no carry-out."

Becky hefted herself off the sofa. "Take most of the omelet. I'm really not very hungry." She sat down and looked at the puffy yellow omelet flecked with specks of green pepper and mushrooms. "Looks good though." She tasted a corner. "Tastes good. Maybe you and I can open a breakfast house. What could they do to chickens?" she joked bitterly.

After eating in silence, Becky did the dishes while Kevin flipped around the TV dial, looking for an old movie to distract them from their gloomy thoughts.

"Are you interested in watching 'The Zucchini That Ate Cincinnati'?" he chuckled. "I'll have to admit a certain addiction to old horror movies. They're so bad they're good."

"I could use some fantasy horror," Becky remarked dryly as she reentered the living room.

Kevin sat at the end of the sofa. "Come lie down and put your head in my lap so you won't get too scared," he grinned.

Doing as she was told, Becky looked up at Kevin with a small, wry smile. "Hard to imagine anything that could scare me much after the past month."

Kevin leaned down to kiss her tenderly. Stroking her hair, he settled in to watch the movie, but part of his mind was searching for a way to approach Becky again about talking with Leo. Kevin was certain Leo was the link between them and the source of the PCBs. Very probably the source of all their other troubles, for that matter. He wouldn't bring it up tonight while Becky was so vulnerable, but she would have to consider it tomorrow.

He studied the fine bones in her face, the tiny lines around her mouth and eyes that were laughter's legacy, the soft curves of her sleeping kitten body, and his love for this woman filled every hidden corner of his mind and soul. For a moment, his hands fairly itched for the throat of the unseen adversary assaulting her so ruthlessly. Don't get mad, get even, he reminded himself. Tomorrow they had to go see Leo.

Becky stirred under his arm. "Kevin, I don't think I'm going to make it much past the outskirts of Cincinnati," she said in a tiny voice muzzy with sleep.

"Listen, I think we'd better go see Leo tomorrow, don't you?"

"I think that's a good idea, honey," Kevin said with a nod. "Now go on to sleep if you want to."

"You won't leave me, will you?" She wrapped one arm around his knee.

"In the middle of an exciting movie like this? Not likely," he chuckled, squeezing her shoulders.

Becky drifted off to sleep, the vibration of Kevin's wonderful chuckle tickling her scalp and his hand draped comfortably over her shoulder, fingertips resting on her breast as lightly as a lover's dream.

Kevin sat before the flickering screen, smiling in relief. Leo might not be able to tell them anything but who his boss was, who sent him to buy the fish, maybe where they were taken, but that might put them in a position to try running a little bluff. It was worth a try, anyway. After all, they didn't have a lot left to lose.

They met with the investigators at Gene's house the next morning. The EPA inspector reported United Industries had no access to PCBs. "As a matter of record, none of your area industries use them."

Kevin frowned impatiently. "But nearly anyone can get their hands on PCBs, if they know where to look."

"That's probably true. There are plenty of old transformers lying around the countryside, but you'd have to know what you were doing." He looked a little discomfited. "You really believe this was a malicious act, don't you?"

"Yes, I do." Kevin's eyes were icy. "What else can I

believe? Have you found any evidence to indicate PCBs got into those ponds to kill those fish?''

"No, we haven't," the inspector admitted. "The tests aren't completed, but we're beginning to believe you may be right. However, what you and I believe is a hell of a long ways from proving anything like that. Unless we can find someone who'll spill his guts to us, or unless we luck out and stumble across the source of the toxin and some evidence linking the fish to that site, we're nowhere. It could take months of scouring the countryside for something like that, and we might never find it. Let's face it, the longer it takes, the more time somebody has to cover his tracks."

"We may know somebody…" Kevin started to say when Becky kicked him under the table, interrupting with a question of her own.

"What about the quarantine?" she asked hastily.

The health inspector shrugged. "I expect we'll lift it in a few days, unless we find something drastically different from what we've found so far."

Becky sighed loudly. "Not that it matters much. After that newspaper article, I doubt customers will be beating a path to our trout. Do you also have to talk to reporters when you don't find anything?" She smiled sweetly.

The investigators excused themselves to get back to work. Becky poured more coffee for herself and Kevin. Gene held his hand over his cup as she offered more to him.

Kevin swung his leg from under the table and rubbed his shin. "What was that for?"

"Leo might talk to me, Kevin, but he certainly

wouldn't talk to any of those guys. No sense bringing it up with them until after we check it out." She turned to Gene. "Dad, did Leo say where he's working?"

"No, not that I recall. Why do you ask?"

"Kevin thinks Leo may know something about all this," she explained, "so we want to talk to him."

"Leo?" Gene asked skeptically.

Kevin quickly outlined his theory about Leo as middle man. "He might lead us to the man we're really looking for."

Gene shook his head ruefully. "Poor old Leo. You know, he pretty much takes at face value what people tell him, especially if he works for them. He could be right square in the middle of it and never know what's going on."

Picking up the phone book, Becky asked, "Do you happen to know where he lives?"

"Don't know that either," Gene said. "I think he's married, and I don't think they're on the old home place."

Becky found Leo's name in the phone book. "Highway 27 West. That's a big help."

Gene brightened. "Listen, when Frank brings the mail today, I'll ask him. That's his old route, and he knows everybody in this neck of the woods. By the way, none of the other trout farms in the area have sold any live trout lately, and I called them all."

The number Becky dialed rang, but no one answered. "Nobody home. Probably they both work in town. Kevin, if Frank knows where Leo lives, let's drive out and see him after work today."

"Okay with me. What time does the mail come?"

Checking his watch, Gene predicted an hour or so wait. They continued drinking coffee and visiting about Kevin's research project until Gene spotted the familiar red truck coming up the road. "There's Frank. I'll be right back." He hurried to intercept the mail carrier, taking the bundle of mail Frank handed him and leaning on the truck window for what seemed to Becky and Kevin a long time. When he finally waved Frank off and returned to the house, they met him at the door. "Well?"

"Well, you can't hurry Frank, you know," Gene grinned. "I had to hear who's having babies, whose cows are sick and other vital gossip. But after all that, I did find out that Leo lives in a trailer stuck back in the woods over on Round Mountain, off the lake road." He retrieved an advertising circular from the bundle. "Here, Frank drew me a map."

Becky kissed her father on the cheek. "Terrific. If he works at a plant, he ought to be home by four o'clock, wouldn't you think?"

"I'd think so." Gene nodded. "And while you're waiting, I have a little chore you can help me with...."

At three-thirty, Becky glanced at her watch and waded out of the cold pond. "Dad, is it okay if we take the truck? Best I remember, those roads on Round Mountain are pretty hard on a car." At Gene's wave, she and Kevin piled into the truck and started out. They were hardly out of the driveway before Becky said, "Kevin, I'd like for you to stay in the truck while I talk to Leo, okay? Sometimes you look pretty scary when the topic turns to fish kills."

He looked at her skeptically for a moment. "Well, Leo certainly isn't the one I'd like to scare, so okay."

Map in hand, Becky directed Kevin to turn off Highway 27 onto a dirt road leading up the mountain into a forest of scrub oak trees. The truck bounced over the rutted road, scrambling for footing on the rocks exposed by repeated washing during heavy rains. Here and there, a lane turned into the trees, leaving a mailbox to show its passing, and made its way to a house half-hidden by summer's foliage.

"I see why you wanted to bring the truck," Kevin observed, dodging a deep rut. "Doesn't look like the county road graders get up this way very often."

"Not much tax money comes off this mountain," Becky commented.

The road narrowed, then dead-ended before an old mobile home, its paint faded to a chalky blue, set up on native stone piers. Someone had carved a vegetable garden out of the woods on one side of the trailer. By the front door two halves of a tractor tire lay as flat flower boxes, enthusiastically sprouting marigolds and zinnias in rainbow colors. As she got out of the truck, Becky noticed homemade bird feeders and a rack of birdhouse gourds stationed nearby. She remembered how Leo enjoyed watching the herons catch trout before Gene put the nylon lines above the ponds. He knew they were flying away with profit, but he always watched with a smile.

At the sound of the truck, a woman appeared at the trailer door, a small child peering around her legs. She watched as Becky got out of the truck, then turned away as Leo came to the door. As he recognized Becky, a surprised smile lit his face. "Becky, what are you doin' out here in the middle of nowhere?" He ambled down the steps to meet her in the yard.

"Hi, Leo. I came to see if you could help me with something," she said, wondering exactly how to get to what she needed to know.

"Well, I will if I can."

"I know." Becky smiled. "Where are you working these days, Leo?"

"Out at United Industries. I'm in maintenance." He kicked at one of the ubiquitous rocks in his yard. "I do mostly janitor work, but other odds and ends of things, too. It's a pretty good job, and I get some overtime now and again."

Becky took a deep breath. "Leo, I have to ask you something, and I don't know how to do it other than just blurting it out. If I'm wrong, I'm sorry, but if I'm right, I think you can help Dad and me a lot."

"Just say it, Becky. I'd like to help your dad any way I could. You know that." His face was open, waiting.

"Leo, we've had two fish kills in the past month. We've traced what caused them to a sludge pond at United Industries. Do you know about that pond, Leo?"

A worried look settled over Leo's face. He chewed his lower lip and kicked another rock with the toe of his boot. "Yeah, I do, Becky, but Charley told me it wasn't nothin' that would hurt anything. He even said it couldn't be what killed your fish, because it was too far away. I asked him about it after I heard about the fish, and that's what he said."

Charley! Like a zoom lens, Becky's memory focused

on that name above a shirt pocket, atop a burly chest, and an unpleasant face threatening her. She forced herself to speak calmly, kindly. "Leo, I know you would never do anything you knew would hurt the fish, but I need to know more about Charley. What can you tell me about him?"

"I don't know as I ought to say anything, Becky. I'd hate to lose my job...."

Time to bring in the big guns, Becky decided. "Leo, on Saturday night, someone dumped some dead fish into our ponds. They'd been killed with a terrible poison that only takes one drop to kill a whole pondful of trout. We think those fish were the ones you bought Friday for your boss."

Leo's eyes were those of a deer poised for flight. "No, Becky, they wouldn't do somethin' like that. Those fish were for the boss's grandkids. I know they were, because Charley told me when he sent me...." He stopped, a realization dawning as he heard his own words.

"Leo, just tell me about Charley and the sludge pond," Becky persisted patiently, "and anything else you know about that might help us. If we're wrong, we'll never say a word about it to anyone. No one will know you talked to me." She saved her strongest plea for last. "Leo, they've quarantined the farm. Dad can't sell any fish, and my restaurant is closed. We stand to lose everything Dad has worked thirty years to build."

The struggle subsided in Leo's face. "I'll tell you what I know, Becky, but I still don't think Charley or Mr. Price would do anything like you're sayin' they did."

"If they didn't, then you can help clear them, Leo," Becky said quietly. "If they did, they need to pay for it. Before you begin, would it be okay if my friend in the truck came to listen? He's been helping us since the first kill."

Leo nodded, and Becky waved to Kevin to join them. Leo waited until Kevin reached them, took a deep breath and said, "Well, the first time was a few weeks ago. Me and Charley went out late at night and hooked up a pipe to get rid of some of the stuff in that pond. It was gettin' too full, and Charley said it wasn't anything that'd hurt to just dump. Said that's how everybody was doin' it since the city tightened up on 'em."

Kevin stood like a carved statue, determined to do nothing to discourage the best source they'd found. Becky urged Leo to continue. "That was our first kill. What about the second time?"

"Well, we done the same thing. That's when I asked Charley about your fish, but he said if the creek don't run into your farm, how was it gonna kill any fish? I couldn't figure any way, so I just let it go by."

"It went through the hillside in a big crack, Leo, and into the pond, we think," Becky explained. "That accounts for the two kills. Now, Leo, what did you do with the fish you bought from us Friday?"

Leo frowned. "I took 'em to Charley, and he said he was takin' truck and all out to the boss's place. Charley says Mr. Price has a real nice acreage south of town. It's part of the old VanMeter place, I think. Becky, you know where that is, don't you?" At her nod, he continued. "Anyhow, I guess he took 'em on out there. I went on back to work and never heard no more about 'em until you got here."

"Charley didn't say anything later about what he did with the fish?" Becky asked hopefully.

Leo shook his head. "The only thing he said was he did another special job for the boss on Saturday night. Said he got a real good bonus for it, but didn't say what it was."

"Leo, you've been very helpful. You're a good friend to Dad and me." Becky smiled. "If it turns out Charley or Mr. Price were responsible for killing our fish, you may have to tell your story to some people from the state who are investigating the whole thing. Okay?"

Leo looked doubtful. "I sure would hate to lose my job, Becky. It's the best I've ever had."

For the first time, Kevin spoke in a soft, steely voice. "Don't you worry, Leo. We'll make sure you don't lose your job over this."

Heading back down the mountain, Kevin asked, "Do we tackle Charley next? He sounds like the real middle man."

Thinking about her close call in the woods, Becky opted for another course. "Let's go around him and head for the top. If Price contaminated those fish, he had to have a holding tank for them until Charley could dump them. Why don't we swing by his place and see if we find anything interesting?"

"Do you know where he lives?"

"We can find it," she said confidently, directing him south to the exclusive housing develpment which included the old VanMeter place Leo mentioned. They drove past several large, ostentatiously expensive houses sitting on manicured tracts of land ranging from two acres to enough land to support a herd of cattle. "Folks who run plants sure live better than folks who work in them, wouldn't you say?" she remarked caustically as she scanned mailboxes for the name she sought. At the last large house she saw a sleek enameled mailbox with the name D. Price painted in Old English script. "There, Kevin."

"We'll circle past and walk back," he said, turning the truck. Pastureland with scattered trees stretched away from the colonial house with its swimming pool and greenhouse. The perimeter of the place was marked by an expensive rail fence. At the end of the fence, they found they could no longer see the house. "This should do." He stopped the truck. "Let's do a little more trespassing."

"You certainly are getting daring in your old age," Becky gibed as she followed him over the fence. They stopped to scan the area where a row of trees marked the passage of a creek. "Look, Kevin." She pointed to a cattle tank gleaming dully in the afternoon sun.

When they reached the tank, they could see it was full of oily-looking water, but there was nothing to indicate it had held fish. "Well, as long as we're here, we might as well take a sample," Kevin said, pulling a bottle out of his shirt pocket and filling it from the tank. "Let's prowl around a little more."

They circled the tank, looking for anything that might connect it to their theory. Becky's foot connected with something solid hidden in the tall grass. "Ouch," she yipped in pain. "What the hell is that doing here? That would wreak havoc with a mowing machine.''

Kevin came to look at the twisted metal object to which she referred. "Becky, you've stumbled on it again. Do you know what this is? It's the remains of an old transformer that's been broken. That's how he did it. He put the fish in the tank and dumped the oil from this transformer in with them.''

The missing pieces of the puzzle began to appear in the proper places. "This is what the EPA investigator needs. Let's go get him," Becky urged.

They started for the road, then Kevin stopped abruptly. "Becky, you go get the investigators. I'll stay here, just in case our friends are planning to get rid of the evidence.''

Becky regarded him with alarm. "Kevin, what will you do if they show up? You can't stay here to face them alone.''

"The sooner you leave, the less chance I'll have to face them alone, Becky," he reminded her hurriedly, "but if they do show up, I'll improvise. We can't afford to lose this stuff. It's the only proof we have. Go!''

Kevin watched as she raced for the truck and listened to its screaming engine as she drove away. He looked at his watch, figuring it would take a minimum of thirty minutes for her round trip. He imagined that would be a long wait in his precarious situation, so he sat on the ground and leaned against a tree, within sight of the evidence but not visible to anyone approaching through the pasture.

His wait was shorter than he'd suspected. He heard a truck coming through the pasture. Knowing it couldn't be Becky, he slipped behind a tangled shrub to watch. The truck backed up to the tank and two men got out. One was a heavyset man in his sixties, his expensive casual clothes contrasting with the heavy rubber gloves extending to his elbows. The other man wore a uniform and similar gloves. As the second man picked up the wrecked transformer to toss it into the truck, Kevin left his hiding place and started for them.

Chapter Fourteen

Her watch showed ten minutes past five as Becky careened into the driveway at Rainbow Ribbon, hoping the investigators would still be there. If they weren't, she had already decided she would call the sheriff to impound the evidence, but the government cars still sat in the parking lot. Becky burst through the back door of her parents' house to find everyone seated in the kitchen drinking coffee. At her appearance, she was bombarded with questions. "Where have you been? Where's Kevin? Gene says you may have an eyewitness. Where is he?"

Becky held up both hands for quiet. "There's not time for that now. We have to get back to...."

Before she could finish her sentence, a knock on the doorframe pulled her around to see Janice Miller peering through the door. "Anybody home? I almost made it by quitting time, didn't I?"

"Janice, what are you doing here?" Becky asked in surprise, nearly forgetting for the moment her errand.

"After I read the lab reports this morning, I decided this would be a good field trip, so I hopped on a plane and came on up," Janice explained. "How's it going, gentlemen?" she asked the inspectors.

"Janice," Becky interrupted, "Kevin and I found the place where they killed the fish, and we have evidence to prove how they did it. Kevin is out there right now to be sure no one tampers with anything. We have our hard evidence . . . please come back with me."

"What are we waiting for?" Janice said, heading out the back door. "Take the car with the testing equipment in it," she threw over her shoulder as she climbed into the truck beside Becky.

The three inspectors piled into the federal car, and Gene hopped into the truck with Becky and Janice. "I'm worried about Kevin," Gene fretted. "These people play hardball."

Becky didn't want to think about that as she sped back to the Price place with the government car dodging afternoon traffic to keep up with her. As she raced along, Becky briefed Janice on the discovery of the cattle tank where there were no cattle and the broken transformer hidden in the weeds. "Sounds pretty incriminating to me," Janice commented with a lifted eyebrow.

As she stopped the truck beside the rail fence, Janice could see the roof of another truck across the pasture near the cattle tank. "They've come back," Becky shouted, climbing the fence and running toward where she left Kevin. "Hurry!"

The group sprinted after Becky, stopping breathlessly as they saw Kevin standing beside the truck, grinning widely. "What's the rush? Everything's under control here." On the tailgate of the truck sat a man

Becky recognized as Charley rubbing his jaw sullenly, and Douglas Price stood near the cattle tank, a look of abject fear on his jowly face.

While the investigators started combing the area, taking pictures and collecting samples, Becky ran to Kevin. "What happened? I was so worried when I saw the truck."

"Nothing much," Kevin shrugged. "I just interrupted the little cleanup party they'd scheduled for this afternoon. The boss man here thought Charley ought to punch me out, but I persuaded him to rethink that. When Price started telling me how Charley did all the dirty work, Charley confirmed my theory without hesitation." He grinned at Janice. "I think Charley will have a lot of interesting things to say to you folks."

"Good," Janice said vehemently, stalking toward the morose Douglas Price. "Mr. Price, I hope you realize you are not only facing some pretty stiff penalties for willful pollution, you will be liable for some criminal charges." She smiled coldly. "I don't imagine your home office will be pleased with the trouble you're going to be bringing them, will they?"

Price's flat gray eyes stared at Janice with naked rancor. As his lips started to form an epithet, Kevin's voice cracked like a whip. "Price, it's not too late...." The older man lapsed into a sour silence.

"Too late for what?" Becky queried. "What are you threatening him with, Kevin?"

Kevin tried to look innocent. "Well, at one point I suggested he should surrender gracefully, or Charley and I might be forced to toss him in the holding tank until help arrived. To his credit, he saw the reasonableness of my request almost immediately.''

"Kevin!" Becky gasped.

"Such a brief exposure wouldn't have done him any harm," Janice assured her, "but I'm glad he didn't know that."

During this discussion Gene stood watching Douglas Price, some strange emotion playing over his usually genial face. No one noticed when he pulled his cap firmly down on his gray hair, doubled up his fist, and started toward Price, his lips compressed with purpose. "Threaten my little girl and ruin my business, will you?" he gritted as he swung out of right field and landed a substantial blow to the more solid of Douglas Price's double chins. As his target crumpled to the ground in shock and pain, Gene turned away, clutching his right hand and groaned in agony.

Kevin roared with laughter. Becky rushed to her father. "Dad, whatever possessed you? I've never heard of you lifting a hand to anybody in your life." She looked at his hand, which was already swelling.

Gene grimaced with a mixture of pain and satisfaction. "Darlin', there are people in this world who beg to be poked in the nose, and he's one of them. I might never have another chance like this." He moaned again, holding the hand against his shirt.

Smothering a laugh, Becky examined the hand gently. "Your aim is as bad as your technique, Rocky. You not only missed his nose, I think you've broken your hand." She turned to Kevin with a long-suffering smile. "I guess I'd better get him to the emergency room, or he'll never play the piano again."

"I don't play the piano now, smart aleck," Gene grumbled, "but it is beginning to smart quite a lot, so I'll go quietly."

"I'll ride back with the inspectors when they're finished," Kevin said. "Janice can go with you."

Janice and Becky helped Gene over the fence and to the truck. As they drove toward the hospital, Becky giggled. At Janice and Gene's quizzical looks, she shared her private joke. "Dad, I can hardly wait to hear you explaining this to Mother. I can just see her now..." she said, imitating her mother's voice, "Gene Sherman, have you taken leave of your senses? An old man like you out acting like a teenager?"

Gene groaned. "All right, all right. No need for putting me through it twice, is there? I'll bet Price won't feel so great in the morning, either," he grumped, nearly drowned out by the women's laughter as they pulled into the hospital lot.

"I'll have to make more field trips to this part of the state," Janice remarked blissfully as she took her first bite of the gourmet trout dinner Sheila and Becky had prepared at Rainbow's End for the inspectors and the family. Gene's right hand was in a cast, and Frances was fussing nearly nonstop, cutting up his food, even trying to feed him.

"Sure is good to hear laughter in here again," Sheila pronounced and smiled at Becky. "And I'm glad you like our food, Janice, but I've missed out on all the fun parts of this thing. Tell me what's going to come of all Becky and Kevin's sleuthing?"

Reluctantly Janice laid down her fork. "I'll call the

main office of United Industries tomorrow, and I imagine Mr. Price will be unemployed by tomorrow evening. He's near retirement, I think, but I suspect his pension will stay with his job to help defray the costs he's incurred for the company. We'll lay some stiff fines on the company and on him individually and make them clean up that pond. The waste hauler providing him with phony paperwork will be put out of business. I'll also talk to the District Attorney tomorrow about possible criminal charges against Price."

As Janice resumed eating, Becky leaned back in her chair, shaking her head. "I don't really understand why he did it, Janice. It would have been cheaper in the long run to dispose of the stuff legally."

"Of course it would, but he never thought he'd get caught, Becky." Janice sighed. "Douglas Price is from the old school. He refuses to accept restrictions on what he sees as a necessary operation, getting rid of excess industrial wastes. He still thinks there's nothing much wrong with dumping. I imagine he's not crazy about having been caught at it." Janice sipped at the white wine before her. "In general, I believe industry is becoming more conscientious about their responsibility to the environment. I'm not sure United's home office would have approved overtly of Price's tactics if they had known what he was doing. I also suspect, however, the home office asks more often about a plant's profit margin than about its waste management practices, so they're not blameless, either."

"It seems to me the man has some serious character flaws," Frances offered. "His actions went beyond preserving his profit. He was spiteful and—and, well, he's obviously just not a nice man," she finished firmly.

Janice's laugh pealed like a deep bell. "I won't argue with that, Mrs. Sherman. As he got in deeper and deeper, his flawed character, as you say, betrayed him." She started to take a bit of the wild rice and stopped the fork halfway to her mouth. "Oh, did I tell you the inspectors found the outlet pipe this afternoon, Becky?"

With a disgusted look, Becky said, "No. I wish you'd tell me how they found it. I looked everywhere for that damned pipe."

"For one thing, they had the advantage of daylight," Janice chuckled. "They found where Charley had removed the valve below the pond, and about twenty feet down the hillside, they located a buried pipe. As you suspected, a length of pipe was brought in to connect the two. We dumped dye in the buried pipe and checked the creek. Pretty as you please, here comes the dye bubbling up through the gravel they'd used to bury it." She turned to Gene. "By the way, if you see any bright blue trout in the morning, Kevin's theory about the fault is validated."

"What will happen to Charley?" Becky wondered aloud.

"Probably nothing, since he's providing most of the evidence against Price and United. I imagine the DA will make a deal with him for immunity, since he has so many useful things to say," Janice guessed.

"And Leo?" Becky asked quietly.

Janice patted her hand. "So far as we're concerned, Leo isn't involved in this. Charley's testimony leaves us with no need for Leo to come into it."

"I'm glad to hear that," Gene nodded. "Leo's still a good boy. He came through for us in the pinch."

Sheila set her wineglass down. "This is all terrific, but I have a vested interest in Rainbow's End. How are we going to undo the damage Price did to the restaurant business we've worked for years to build?"

"I have a couple of ideas about that, too." Janice gestured with her empty fork. "First of all, I called the governor's press aide, and she is in the process of creating a folk heroine. Becky will be living proof of what one person, with a little help from her friends"—she winked—"can do to keep industry honest and preserve this state's relatively unspoiled environment. I want industry to know how serious we are about it, and I want every citizen to see how they can help us." She looked at Sheila, a smile playing at the corners of her mouth. "As for Rainbow's End, I should think the governor would respond favorably if invited to the grand reopening of a folk heroine's recently endangered restaurant."

Amid applause, Sheila suddenly looked stricken. "Oh my goodness. If the governor comes, I'll have to clean this place from top to bottom."

"If you serve him food like this, he'll never notice a little dust," Janice assured her, trying to finish her food between questions. "Kevin, I looked over Gordon's plan for the new sewage plant today. It looks good, and I think the state and federal funds should cover nearly seventy-five percent of the cost, provided industry implements the pretreatment plans Gordon says you've championed all along."

"I imagine they'll be a little more cooperative after the publicity over United," Kevin chuckled.

"I ran into Mrs. Trimble in the grocery store this

afternoon," Frances said. "She nearly assaulted me, said we were responsible for Milam's not running for reelection in November, and she didn't know what they were going to do. I told her he could try working for a living like the rest of us."

Laughter rippled around the table. "Gordon did say something about a leak to the press regarding the mayor's complicity in the incident," Janice recalled smugly.

Sheila stood, holding her wineglass aloft. "I'd like to propose a toast to friends who are the gold at this Rainbow's End."

"And I want all your autographs on my cast, too," Gene directed. "This trophy is going over my fireplace."

Sheila drove Janice to the airport for a late flight, and the inspectors left to start the tediously effective paperwork that would bring the case to a satisfactory conclusion.

"Kevin, I want to thank you for all the help you've been to us during this thing," Gene said, his blue eyes deep and sincere. "It's cost you your job and Lord knows what else, but it's meant a lot to us."

"What about me?" Becky teased her dad. "I did a few pretty important things, too, even if I didn't slug anybody."

"I never doubted what you could do in self-defense," Gene grinned. "After all, you inherited my charm and your mother's grit, didn't you?" He wrapped his bandaged hand around Becky's waist and clasped Kevin's shoulder with his good hand. "Kevin, you'll find that to be quite a combination. I expect we'll continue to see you around a lot, won't we?'' he asked, his eyes twinkling with mischief. ''I'd say more than one of the Shermans has gotten pretty attached to you over the last month.''

Becky hugged her dad and kissed her mother on the cheek. ''Mother, take this old daredevil home and confine him to his recliner until he comes to his senses. We'll take care of everything here.''

Walking out with the older couple, Kevin and Becky watched them down the hill, then turned down the path to their overlook. It seemed a lifetime since their first evening together there. Kevin kissed her warmly. ''I think this time it really is over, sweetheart.''

Her arms clasped around his waist, Becky leaned back to look into his smiling face. ''There were times I thought we'd never be able to say that. Without your help, we might not be saying it now.''

Kevin's fingertips traced a line from her temple to her chin. He chuckled at the memory of their first meeting. ''Hard to remember I saw you as the bearer of a problem more interesting than the city could offer.''

Becky tugged at his beard. ''And now that the problem is solved, will you be riding off into the sunset to search for newer and bigger problems to tackle?''

''Well, that sort of depends on you. You're pretty settled here, aren't you?''

''Yes, but . . . .''

''I have an old-fashioned idea about married people sharing the same domicile, so if you'll marry me, the sun will have to set on my back.'' He smiled crookedly.

Becky withdrew her hands from Kevin's waist and

stepped back to regard him solemnly. "Kevin, are you serious? What about your career? Are you sure you haven't had too much to drink today?"

"An Irishman has never had too much to drink so long as he can grasp a blade of grass to keep from sliding off the edge of the world," he recited broadly, stooping to pinch off a green stem at his feet. "See? Of course I'm serious. I love you, Becky. I like this area, and if something doesn't turn up through the university, which I think it will, I can set up a lab anywhere. I think Janice Miller would be a good reference, don't you?" He cocked his head to one side. "Well, any other questions before you say yes?"

Becky's face rivaled the full moon for splendor. "No. I mean, yes. Yes, I'll marry you, you crazy Irishman." She threw her arms around his neck and kissed him soundly. "I love you, too. I tried to imagine what I'd do if you said you were leaving, and I couldn't even face thinking about it. It'd be dumb to break up an act as good as this one, wouldn't it?" She grinned at him. "Dad is going to be very pleased about this, you know. He likes you a lot, and he'll be getting some good help in the bargain," she giggled.

"What about your mother?" Kevin asked tentatively.

"Honey, she'll be so glad I've finally come to my senses and found a good man, she won't know what to do. She likes you personally, but that's just a bonus." She looked at Kevin, her turquoise eyes glowing. "Maybe we'd better run away to get married. As long as I've made Mother wait, she may take six months just planning the wedding."

Kevin laughed. "No going over the wall, dear heart. We'll just tell her I'm allergic to large groups, so she'll need to limit the invitations to the number of people who can stand comfortably around this rock and still see us by the light of my oil lamp."

"That should do it." Becky giggled in delight. "Hey, you didn't bring your lamp tonight?"

The moonlight tipped his hair to match his silver eyes. "No night will never be dark enough to hide you from the eyes of my heart," he whispered dramatically.

"Kevin, that's beautiful. Is it another of your old Irish sayings?" she murmured, kissing his ear softly.

"Let's just say it'll be old before I have need to say anything else," he said, his hungry soul heading for the home he saw in her eyes.